And Did Murder Him

Previous books by Peter Turnbull

PETER TURNBULL

And Did Murder Him

A Glasgow P Division procedural

St. Martin's Press
New York

Library of Congress Cataloging-in-Publication Data

Turnbull, Peter.
    And did murder him / Peter Turnbull.
        p.   cm.
    ISBN 0-312-05813-6
    I. Title.
PR6070.U68A84   1991
823'.914—dc20   90-28440
                                                                 CIP

First published in Great Britain by William Collins Sons & Co. Limited.

First U.S. Edition: August 1991
10 9 8 7 6 5 4 3 2 1

And Did Murder Him

CHAPTER 1

Sunday, 08.00–10.45 hours

Sunday morning in the city of Glasgow. Wide thoroughfares are empty, there is trash from the night before, empty cans, pizza wrappers, remnants of fish suppers, pools of dried vomit in the doorways. A van is driving; periodically it stops, the driver's mate leaps from the cab and carries a bundle of newspapers which he leaves on the pavement in front of shops, or perhaps he hands them to a street vendor setting up his pitch. There are buses, a few, mostly empty. A milk-float rattles by. It is mid-March, at the end of what had been a particularly mild winter. The sky is still grey, but it will become blue. It is dry, a day for a pullover and jacket. A good walking day for a rambler. But this is the city, it is the grid system at the centre, angular buildings, solid Victorian and Georgian buildings standing on wide streets, streets which intersect each other at ninety degrees, streets with strong, solid names—St Vincent, Regent, Bath, Sauchiehall, Hope. A man is walking.

The man walked up Bath Street from Charing Cross. He walked with a slow, even pace, observing as he went, and allowing himself to savour the tranquillity of the morning. At the summit of Bath Street, he turned into Blythswood Square and enjoyed the spectacle of the rising sun shining on the stone-cleaned Georgian façades of the buildings on the north side of the square. He paused at the first corner of the square, he just stood for two or three minutes, allowing himself to be seen; reinforcing his presence.

The man's name was Hamilton. He was twenty-four years old. He was a cop.

Hamilton was working the day shift. He wanted it to be quiet. Sundays mostly are. Mostly.

He walked round to southern and eastern sides of

5

Blythswood Square, in front of the National Westminster Bank and the RAC Building, and down towards Sauchiehall Street. On impulse, he turned into the Sauchiehall Lane alley which ran behind Sauchiehall Street.

Sauchiehall Lane was deserted. It stretched in front of Hamilton, a narrow straight canyon, cobbled surface and high walls with steel doors set in them, heavy metal grilles over the windows, and barbed wire coiled round the drainpipes. The lane assumed a gentle incline to a summit some three hundred yards from the point that Hamilton entered, whereupon it fell in an equally gentle decline to West Nile Street. At intervals along the length of the alley were small 'inshots' in the lane at buildings where cars were parked during the day, many boldly labelled 'private parking only'. As in the main streets, Sauchiehall Lane had collected indications of the revelry that is Glasgow town on a Saturday night; half-empty super-lager cans; half-eaten pizzas; fish supper wrappers screwed up and tossed aside; pools of dried vomit; a car in a private parking bay with the smashed side window and the hi-fi torn from the fascia; the corpse.

The corpse lay in the Lane close to its entrance at West Nile Street; it lay crumpled in a doorway. In life he had been a boy of perhaps nineteen years; he had been of medium stature, a small face of pointed and pinched features. He had thin hair which he wore long over his eyes and down to his shoulders. He was dressed in denim, patched and torn, a shirt, a pair of soiled and worn training shoes. All this Hamilton noted with a glance as he reached for his radio, as he spoke into the handset which was clipped to the collar of his uniform: '. . . assistance required, Sauchiehall Lane and West Nile Street. Apparent Code 41 . . .' Hamilton's call was acknowledged by a crisply spoken female officer and he then switched off the handset. He looked at the body. It was his impression that the youth had not the deliberate designer slovenliness of a student; rather he had the desperate grinding one-day-at-a-time slovenliness of the chronically unemployed, or unemployable, or of the mentally ill or of the drug-abuser, the murders of whom always seem to outnumber the murders of those in the mainstream of life, and the murders of whom

6

invariably seem to be cheap, grubby and impulsive. Just as this fatality appeared to be. He knelt. The body was cold. No pulse. Dead.

The body lay in a recessed doorway, hidden mostly from view and could well have lain undiscovered until much later in the day had not Hamilton decided to patrol the lane instead of the street.

Hamilton walked to the nearer end of Sauchiehall Lane, and stood on the pavement of West Nile Street, leaving the body undisturbed just as he had found it, fifteen feet behind him. He watched an orange bus go by, the only vehicle on the street at that time on that Sunday morning and empty save for one or two passengers downstairs. Hamilton thought: nineteen years, Sauchiehall Lane, in March, a grubby way to die, knifed to death, the black bloodstains on the shirt attested to that. He heard a klaxon pierce the silence; it grew closer and a police car, a white saloon 'sandwich car' turned into West Nile Street and drew to a halt beside Hamilton.

'Just here,' said Hamilton as the two officers got out of the car. 'Behind, here in the Lane.'

The two mobile patrol officers moved with an efficiency which Hamilton had seen before, but which still impressed him. They quickly erected an orange tape across the entry of the alley and then drove the vehicle round to Renfield Street at the other side of the block to cordon off the other entrance to the alley. Hamilton remained with the corpse, at the locus of the offence. Within three minutes the car had returned to where Hamilton waited, with the driver as the only occupant. The driver left the vehicle, allowing the blue revolving light to remain switched on.

'That's the alley sealed off.' The driver stood next to Hamilton. 'Some way to start a Sunday!'

'Some way to start any day,' said Hamilton, glancing behind him at the crumpled youth; no money in life, no dignity in death. But at least his eyes were closed.

Tuesday Noon walked home. Staggering, swaying, too much wine in the night, stayed up through the night, walked home through the city. Saw a cop, walking up Bath Street, saw him turn into Blythswood Square; Tuesday Noon ducked into a doorway, didn't want to be seen, not in this condition, drunk and disorderly, a walking target for any keen young cop wanting to boost his arrest rate. He waited until the police officer disappeared from view and then continued to walk on.

The blue car swept by, shooting red lights at seventy or eighty miles an hour.

Tuesday Noon watched the car intently, curiously. He recognized the vehicle. He recognized the driver.

Ray Sussock had drawn the day shift that weekend, the last weekend before Easter. Saturday had been hectic, burglaries, shoplifting, FAX inquiries from police forces south of the border concerning Scottish drug barons who were moving about the Home Counties with increasing degrees of suspiciousness. It had been a full day, but routine; a succession of small jobs, light work, handed over to Richard King who had drawn the back shift. Home, briefly, to a bedsitter in the West End, and then to Langside for a meal and the remainder of the night spent with her in her neat, warm room and kitchen. The Sunday morning had dawned dull, but dry, and he left her flat at 6.30 and drove to P Division police station at Charing Cross, stopping en route to buy the Sunday papers. He arrived at P Division at 7.0 a.m., signed in, checked his pigeonhole for messages, climbed the stairs to the CID corridor, sat with Montgomerie who had worked the night shift and had not, it seemed to Sussock, been at all overworked given the amount of work he handed over; really only a spate of car thefts and thefts from cars. In respect of the latter, it seemed that the thieves had stolen a red Fiesta from the car park of the Queen Mother's Hospital and had worked their way from car park to car park all over the West End, moving it seemed to the police who followed the spoor, in a rough direction towards the city centre, whereupon the break-ins stopped being reported and the trail went cold.

'Found the stolen vehicle half an hour ago,' said Montgomerie, looking bleary-eyed and with a shadow of growth about his neat jaw. 'But no trace of the twenty-odd stereos that have been stolen from cars, and those are just the twenty that have been reported. I would guess another twenty will be reported in the course of the day. Also,' continued Montgomerie, 'you'll see in the recording that one car belonged to a climber; his ice-pick was stolen, and another car belonged to someone who was a keen country dancer; he lost the ceremonial swords used in the sword dance.'

'So there's some handy weapons floating about,' said Sussock, the much older of the two officers. He picked up the file and put it to one side.

'Car is being dusted for prints right now,' said Montgomerie as an afterthought, 'but I dare say we'll find that they wore gloves.'

'So TV can teach something.'

'More's the pity.' Montgomerie reached for the next file. 'Well,' he said, 'we finally caught her. Felt her pretty little collar just as she stepped off the train at Queen Street, just at the back of eleven last night.'

'Who?'

'Saracen Cynthia, otherwise known as Cynthia McGarvie of Stoneyhurst Street. She was spotted by a WPC who acted "on suspicion", as is said.'

'Bag full of goodies?' asked Sussock.

'Three bagloads full of goodies.' Montgomerie lit a nail, dragged the smoke deep into his lungs. Sussock suddenly recalled the days when he could do that and indeed did so, heavily; now, years later, he felt the thin air of March gripping his chest and stabbing his lungs, being the legacy of years of smoking cigarettes. He no longer smoked but his chest still hurt in the winter months and he always knew when summer was waning, long before the leaves started to fall. The advert for the sports car which read 'Grips like the Scottish winter, goes like the Scottish summer' had special meaning for him.

'Well, you know the story,' said Montgomerie. 'Cynthia got known so well in this town that she had to spread her net, and she hunted and gathered over greater distances. She spent all Saturday afternoon in Stirling, raiding the department stores; she delayed her return, hoping to sneak back up to the Saracen in the wee small hours. She was found to have three bags of shoplifted goods, five hundred quid's worth when we tallied up the price labels. She could have sold it in Possilpark for about two hundred and fifty quid. I gather half the label price is the going rate for the sale of stolen goods in the scheme.'

'Not a bad rate of pay for an afternoon's work.'

'Not bad at all.' Montgomerie tapped ash into the ashtray. 'Anyway, she's in the cells, charged, squealing about the injustice of it all and full of her rights. She'll appear before the Sheriff on Monday, tomorrow.'

'Very good. Not bailed?'

Montgomerie shook his head. 'Last time she jumped bail and fled south, remained submerged for months until she was picked up in London for shoplifting.'

'She'll never learn, and still only eighteen.'

'Unreal. She says it's safer than working the street and pays just as well.' Montgomerie pulled on the cigarette. 'There was a domestic burglary in Hyndland, one hell of a neat job. They had smashed a beautiful stained glass window to gain entry, but after that, it was neat. Stole the video recorder, cameras, watches, but didn't vandalize the house. Some consolation for the home owner, but not much. That's still to be visited by Forensic.'

'All right.'

'And that's about it.' Montgomerie stood. 'It was quiet for the CID. Uniform boys have been busy, cells are crowded with neds with hangovers.'

'Just another Saturday.'

'That's it.' Montgomerie put his coat on. 'Have fun,' he said, and left the room.

Sussock read over the files 'on hold', made coffee, opened the Sunday paper.

His phone rang. He picked it up.

'Sussock.'

'Controller, sir. Code 41. West Nile Street and Sauchie-

10

hall Lane. PC Hamilton and Tango Delta Foxtrot currently in attendance. CID presence requested.'

Sussock paused, absorbing the implications. 'I'm on my way,' he said, and replaced the handset.

'Any ID?' Sussock peered at the body; the pale, wasted look on the dead youth's face was to stay with Sussock for some time. He had the immediate impression that death had made only the slightest alteration to the youth's pallor.

Hamilton confessed that he had not checked for any ID.

'Well, you could look in his jacket pockets without disturbing him too much, could you not?'

Hamilton did so, crouching as he did. He stood and shook his head. 'Nothing at all, Sarge.'

'It was worth a try,' he said, as an orange bus whined down West Nile Street. The police activity was causing passengers' heads to turn. 'The rest of his pockets will have to wait until we get him to the mortuary. That will be a matter of minutes, I'd say. Dr Chan's on his way. He's apparently attending a sudden death in Springburn.'

Hamilton shuffled his feet. 'Two sudden deaths and it's still not nine a.m. And a Sunday, too.'

Sussock scowled at Hamilton. It was not, he thought, not at all like the young constable to be cynical. Behind him, Sussock heard a car door open and shut with a solid thud. The mobile patrol officer had taken a blanket out of the rear of the car.

'It's getting a wee bit public, Sarge,' he said, as he passed Sussock and walked towards the corpse. 'The city's beginning to wake up.' He unfolded the blanket and laid it over the body. The constable had done this before, most probably to victims of road accidents, as is often the lot of mobile patrol officers. Sussock was angry with himself; the action of the officer was something he should have thought of and requested.

Sussock turned and walked to the far end of Sauchiehall Lane. He strolled more than walked, not really undertaking a painstaking inch by inch search of the cobbles and the doorways and the car-parking 'inshots' that he knew would be done later by a team of constables, walking side by side, crouching side by side if necessary, inching forward on their haunches. On this occasion Sussock wanted only to cover the ground from one end of the alley to the other, to conduct a preliminary sweep; he wanted to do something because he should not have had to wait for a uniformed constable to remember to cover the corpse with a blanket. He walked towards the far end of the alley, establishing for himself the nature of the terrain and topography of the locus of the offence, to undertake a brief but wide search, hoping to find something obvious, something relevant . . .

Like a knife.

It was an ordinary five-inch-bladed kitchen knife, with a silver blade and a wooden handle. There is one, or a rack of similar knives, in every home in the city, which fact goes a long way to explaining why the kitchen knife with the five-inch blade is Scotland's number one murder weapon. As in the rest of the western world, murders in Scotland are most often grubby, spontaneous and domestic; an argument in the kitchen between husband and wife can and, in Sussock's long experience, often did escalate until one or other partner reached for a weapon while in a state of uncontrollable anger; a frying-pan, a rolling-pin, a knife . . .

On this occasion the knife lay under the wall of the building on the left side of the alley that was Sussock's left as he walked along with West Nile Street behind him. It lay on the same side of Sauchiehall Lane as did the corpse, by now properly covered by an orange blanket. The knife was stained from the tip of the blade to the hilt with dark, almost black, dried congealed blood. Sussock turned and shouted to Hamilton.

'Productions bag from the car, please.'

Hamilton brought up the bag, a twelve-inch square bag of clear cellophane, self-sealing at the opening.

'Anything, Sarge?' he said, handing the bag to Sussock.

'One knife, laddie.' Sussock kneeled and, taking the knife gingerly between thumb and middle finger, picked it up and placed it in the bag. He folded down the seal and handed the bag to Hamilton.

'Put it in the car, please,' he said. 'And label it, of course.'

'Of course, Sarge,' said Hamilton.

Sussock continued to stroll the length of Sauchiehall Lane, searching the ground from side to side as he did so. He noted muck, empty cans, a dead pigeon torn and savaged probably not by a cat but more likely by a fox, which is not by any means an uncommon sight in Glasgow during the empty hours of the night. He noticed fish supper wrappers, pizza wrappers, used and discarded condoms, signs of attempted entry into buildings, signs of actual entry into a car somewhat recklessly left overnight in the Lane, but he noticed nothing else of obvious relevance or significance to the apparent Code 41 which was the orange mound some two hundred feet behind him. Sussock reached the summit and looked along the remainder of the Lane where he saw the second officer of the mobile patrol standing a lonely guard at the end of the Lane where it was intersected by Renfield Street. Sussock continued to stroll, seeing more clearly as the sky melted from grey to blue; he observed as he went, searching the cobbles, the window-ledges, the doorways, but not actually venturing into the recesses off the Lane where cars were parked mid-week; these, he knew, would be thoroughly searched later in the morning.

Eventually he reached the end of the Lane and stood beside the second officer of the mobile patrol. In front of them Sauchiehall Lane cut a deep canyon, intersecting three more streets until it terminated at Elmbank Street. The entire length would probably be searched, thought Sussock; the position of the knife indicated to him that the murderer had stabbed his victim at the West Nile Street entrance of Sauchiehall Lane and had then run—Sussock presumed he had run—into the Lane rather than up or down West Nile Street, and had escaped into the grid system and into the city at any major road along Sauchiehall Lane from Renfield Street to Elmbank Street. The murderer would have made his way down Sauchiehall Lane at a hell for leather run, or by creeping softly from shadow to shadow to shadow. As he went, running or creeping, but a run Sussock thought would be more likely, he discarded the weapon in a panic. The

13

knife had lain there as if flung away; a man moving stealthily does not do things in a panic. The murder itself seemed to be opportunistic and impulsive, probably as a result of an alcohol-induced frenzy, because anyone who would plan a murder carefully would dispose of the weapon carefully.

So, thought Sussock, as he stood beside the second officer of the mobile patrol, sometime in the night a man or a woman, but probably a man, had run down the alley in a state of panic, and on reaching Renfield Street might have turned left or right, but might equally have run the length of the alley, enjoying the anonymity offered by the shadows, before finally, it could be reasonably assumed, composing himself and stepping into the street lights and walking home, or taking the tube, or a bus, or jumping a cab.

He'd walk.

Sussock would have walked home, no matter where home was. If he had killed a man by stabbing him to death, and presumably getting into a scuffle in the process, then he would need the darkness in order to reach home. He would have the man's blood on his clothes, and the man might have turned and scratched his assailant's face and, if so, not only would he have bloodstained, sweet-smelling clothing, but he would also be scratched about the face. He would be conspicuous among passengers on the bus or the tube. A cab-driver would have driven him straight to the nearest police station. If Sussock had been the murderer he would have walked home, so he reasoned it was not at all unreasonable to assume the actual murderer had walked home.

'We found a knife,' Sussock told the officer, breathing deeply, forcing cold March morning air into his lungs and wincing at the discomfort.

'Really, sir?'

'Gets us off to a good start, anyway.' Sussock exhaled. 'Don't let any member of the public in or out of the lane. I'm sure you wouldn't anyway.'

'Very good, Sarge.'

Sussock turned and retraced his steps. Upon reaching the summit of the Lane, he noticed that a small, blue-suited Oriental gentleman had arrived at the locus and was presently kneeling over the corpse, with Hamilton and the mobile patrol officer holding up the blanket, using it as a screen to shield the corpse from view from any prying eyes on West Nile Street. Dr Chan, the police surgeon, had arrived.

Sussock approached to within ten feet of Dr Chan and then stopped, not wanting to intrude on the work of the police surgeon, or to intrude on his personal space. Dr Chan turned and smiled at Sussock.

'Well, the young man is deceased,' he said. 'I can confirm death.'

'Thank you, sir.'

Dr Chan stood. 'Death appears to be occasioned by stab wounds to the chest, but the pathologist will confirm that, or otherwise. All I can say is that he is deceased.'

'Very good, sir. I'll ask the pathologist to attend. Could you indicate time of death?'

'Within hours, I'd say.' Chan buttoned his jacket. 'Rigor mortis hasn't set in, but the blood is very dry, drier than it should be in the absence of rigor. Really, you'll have to wait for the pathologist's report.'

Sussock glanced at his watch and noted the time for his report. It was 10.15 hours.

Janet Reynolds sat at the breakfast bar in the kitchen of her home. She was a woman in her mid-thirties, attractive, sandy-haired, with a beautifully smooth complexion. She wore a full-length housecoat, carpet slippers, and she sipped her umpteenth cup of coffee that morning while she devoured the review section of the *Sunday Times*. Her home was a spacious, detached villa in Pollokshaws, stone-cleaned, well-maintained, and all-in-all a very desirable property. Outside, in the rear gardens, warm in jeans and sweaters, her two children romped with Gustav, the St Bernard. Upstairs in the master bedroom to the front of the house, her husband still slumbered. In the night, as often happened, he had been awakened by a phone-call from the police requesting his attendance at a suspicious death. On this occasion the phone-call had been made at a little after 02.00

15

hours, and as usual, her husband, a light sleeper, had answered the phone promptly, spoken less than he had listened, replaced the handset and rolled smoothly out of bed; he had dressed outside the bedroom so that he wouldn't awaken her. And as also was usual, she had in fact awakened at the first ring of the phone and had none the less continued to pretend to be asleep so as not to upset him as he tiptoed out of their bedroom with a bundle of his clothing in his arms. She had, as was her habit on such occasions, lain awake as the silver Volvo, with her husband at the wheel, had reversed down the drive, crunching the gravel insisted on by her husband because it was a good burglar deterrent, whining in reverse gear. She had lain in bed listening to the vehicle drive away; first, second, third, fourth gear; always amazed how far sound seemed to travel at night. Only when she was sure that her husband had rounded the distant bend of their road did she turn on the bedroom light.

Janet Reynolds benefited from insomnia.

For many years she had suffered from it. For many years she felt herself to be a misfit, a freak of nature, abnormal and monstrous, because she didn't need eight hours' sleep each twenty-four like everybody else needed. Sometimes, in desperation, she faked it, lying with her eyes closed for six hours until she fell asleep, then slept for two and awoke fully refreshed. In times of greater desperation she attempted, and often succeeded, to induce sleep with the assistance of pills or alcohol, or sometimes, when very desperate, with a dangerous mixture of both. After such attempts she would awaken feeling like a wreck.

Her life changed for her when she was in her late teens. And it changed suddenly. She was doing nothing but walking down the street to the corner shop to buy some groceries when it occurred to her that if she did not need eight hours' sleep every twenty-four then she just didn't need it. Simple. It was as if a large dinner plate which had been held in front of her eyes had suddenly shattered and through the breaking shards a light shone brilliantly and she saw her way forward.

16

Her life changed instantly. She began to like herself and her self-image improved. Instead of seeing herself as having to come to terms with a handicap of some description, she saw herself as being uniquely privileged, believing her life to have greater longevity than most, not in terms of years but in terms of measurable periods of consciousness. She began to study, went to university, where she met the man who was to become her wonderful husband. When their children were young, she survived the very early years better than most young mothers, because she always had up to six hours to herself each and every night which were hers and hers alone, and should one of the children wake during those hours, then she was already awake, active and pleased to respond. In later years, when her children slept through to the night, she would use those hours to study for a master's degree, which she did on a part-time basis; she devoured an enormous amount of literature and taught herself foreign languages.

That Sunday morning she had been awake for six hours before her children began to stir. Her husband slept late, having returned only at 7.30; by 10.0 a.m. the children had breakfasted, had helped with the washing-up and had taken Gustav into the back garden; she had returned to the Sunday papers and to the coffee. She was a happy, content and utterly fulfilled woman.

The phone rang. Janet Reynolds extended a slender arm and picked up the wall-mounted handset.

'Dr Reynolds,' she said.

''Morning, madam,' said a soft-spoken but distinctly West of Scotland female voice, 'Controller, P Division here. Sorry to bother you on Sunday morning, but may I speak to Dr Reynolds, please?'

'Again?' She let the newspaper fall flat on the breakfast bar. 'He only returned from an incident three hours ago. He's still asleep.'

'There really is nobody else we can ask, madam,' said the voice with polite insistence.

'Hold the line, please.' She spoke sharply. She was angry, feeling as deeply the sense of injustice done to her husband as she would feel angry about an injustice done to herself. She left the kitchen, kicking a plastic toy out of her path as she did so, walked down the hall and turned up the wide staircase, turned again on the landing and softly opened the door of the bedroom which she shared with her husband. In the darkened room she saw the silver-haired head of her husband lying on the black pillow case and the sharply patterned red, black and white duvet covering his trim figure. He turned as she opened the door.

'Is that for me?' he asked.

'Uh-huh,' she said, softly, kneeling beside him so that her face was level with his. 'The boys in blue for you. P Division this time. Where's that? Down town or in the sticks?'

'It's in the town.' He levered himself up. 'Smack in the centre.' He reached for the phone by the bed. 'Hello, Reynolds here.'

'I'll grind some fresh beans and grill some bacon.' Janet Reynolds stood and left the room. She was very proud of her husband.

Minutes later he joined her in the kitchen, dressed casually, clean freshly ironed shirt, brown corduroy trousers, soft shoes. He yawned and re-tied his tie. She pressed a mug of coffee into his hands.

'More gore?' she said.

'Apparently so.' Reynolds sipped the steaming fluid. 'Dr Chan has just pronounced death on a young man of nineteen or twenty. A formality, I'd say, given that the cause of death is apparently multiple stab wounds.'

'But that's for you to confirm.' She glanced out of the rear door of her house at her children and Gustav, romping playfully, safely, while a few miles away, a nineteen- or twenty-year-old lay dead of multiple stab wounds. Two worlds in the same city.

'I'll try and get back before midday.' Reynolds blew on the coffee. 'Did I hear you mention bacon?'

'It's grilling.' She smiled. 'As I'm sure you can smell.'

'Excellent. I never like going out on an empty stomach.'

'We said that we'd take the children to the Burrell Collection this afternoon,' she said tentatively, sliding sizzling rashers out of the eye-level grill.

Reynolds paused. 'I think you'll have to go without me. I'm sorry, but that's the way of it sometimes. You might not need your eight hours, but I do.'

Reynolds parked his Volvo close to the entrance of Sauchiehall Lane. He left his car, making a quick mental note of the temperature and the weather conditions. Later he would make exact notes, but as he walked to the entrance of the lane, towards the police car with the blue revolving lights and the uniformed constables and Dr Chan, who stood chatting to the elderly police officer, Sergeant Sussock, it was enough for Reynolds to note that it was dry and perhaps four to five degrees above freezing, no wind, therefore no chill factor to aggravate heat loss. Apparently one of the more simple scenarios. Reynolds also noticed the black mortuary van standing close by, summoned no doubt as soon as Dr Chan had pronounced death. Inside the van the driver and his mate sat with their feet on the dashboard, smoking cigarettes and each reading the *Sunday Mail*. It was, for them, just another stiff to be lifted from the street and taken to the mortuary, like delivering meat. As Reynolds looked at them, the driver's mate wound down his window and tossed his fag-end into the gutter.

Reynolds walked into the alley. He saw a mound covered by an orange blanket.

'So he's dead?' Reynolds spoke to Dr Chan.

'Yes, sir,' said Chan.

'Well, let's have a look at him,' Reynolds said. He had got to know Dr Chan in recent months and knew that Chan liked to stay and observe him work out of a professional interest.

Sussock peeled back the blanket and revealed the crumpled body of the youth.

Reynolds sighed. Like Hamilton earlier, Reynolds saw not just a life savagely cut short when just on the threshold of adulthood, but the sheer wasted, pale, drawn appearance of the young man. The long dirty hair, the thin dirty denims which would offer no protection in the cold, the worn training shoes with ill-matching laces. He knelt by the body and opened the front of the denim jacket and revealed the bloodstained shirt. He opened the shirt and examined the chest.

'Stab wounds,' he said. 'I can see no other evident injury but I'll test for poison as a matter of course. I think, though, that as you say, Dr Chan, the stab wounds will be the cause of death.' Reynolds opened his bag and took a thermometer and noted the air temperature; 4°C, and the time; 10.37 hrs. He noted both in a small pocket notebook.

'Could you suggest a time of death, please, sir?' Sussock asked. 'It would give us something to work on.'

'Hours,' said Reynolds. 'Can't be more certain than that. I think that he was murdered here, not elsewhere, because rigor is apparently just setting in and he's in the position that he would be in if he had been stabbed and left to slump against the wall, rather than been dumped. What do you think it is, a Saturday-night knifing?'

'Most probably, sir,' Sussock replied. 'Cheap and as grubby as they come. I think I've already found the murder weapon.'

'Oh.'

'A kitchen knife.'

'The old perennial, eh?' said Reynolds. 'What is to Glasgow as Colt .45s are to cowboy films. If you'd bring it to the post-mortem, I'll test it on the injuries, see if it fits. I take it that you'll attend?'

'Yes, sir.'

'Excuse me, sir,' said Chan, 'I have no wish to presume upon your field of expertise . . .'

'Go on, please.' Reynolds smiled. He liked Chan.

'Well, it worries me that there is an absence of rigor when the blood seems to be days old. It isn't fresh blood. Also, I think that if he was murdered here, there would be blood on the wall and surface of the alley, yet there is none. It is only a humble observation, sir.'

20

Reynolds looked at Chan with widening eyes. He nodded his head slowly.

'A humble observation you call it, sir?'

It was Sunday, 10.45 a.m.

CHAPTER 2

Sunday, 13.00–17.10 hours

It was a scene that Sussock had witnessed many times before. He was in a room which had industrial grade linoleum on the floor, three blank whitewashed walls, the fourth wall being largely given over to a huge sheet of glass behind which were rows of seats staggered in raised tiers. The room was illuminated by filament bulbs encased in opaque perspex to cut out the 'shimmer' from the bulbs. In the centre of the room stood a stainless steel table which had a one-inch lip around the edge. It was supported by a single pedestal which Sussock knew was hollow in order to allow blood to drain away. A trolley, also of stainless steel, stood beside the table and on it lay rows of surgical instruments. On the table was the corpse which had that morning been found folded and crumpled in thin denim in an alley behind Sauchiehall Street. Now it was laid out, face upwards, arms beside the body. It had been washed down with alcohol and was now naked save for a starched white towel which had been draped over the coyly termed 'private parts' of the body. Dr Reynolds stood beside the table, he had a small microphone attached to the lapel of his smock. Sussock stood reverently in the corner of the room.

He was pleased that the mortuary assistant who was normally in attendance was not present on this occasion. The mortuary assistant was a small man with short, greased-down hair and always seemed to have a sinister gleam in his eyes, especially as he cast them lovingly over

21

corpses. Sussock had always found himself unnerved by this assistant; he seemed to Sussock to be a man who loved his work in the unhealthiest of ways.

When Sussock had first married, in the halcyon days of his life when he and his wife were not just talking to each other, but were actually loving with each other, they had lived for a short while in a two apartment off London Road. In the flat above theirs had lived old Mr Duffy and his wife whom Sussock remembered fondly as a very pleasant couple indeed. Mr Duffy had been a mortuary assistant and his work had destroyed him. When Sussock had known him, Mr Duffy had been in his declining years and he lived every working moment in sheer terror of his own death. Mrs Duffy had to nurse him down the stair, coax him across the road, escort him to the pub, where she would leave him for two hours while she did the shopping and then, having taken the shopping home first, would return to the pub and coax her timid husband back into their house, where he was happy to sit so long as she was there. He was in terror of his own death because he knew, when he died, which van, driven by which man and mate, would arrive and collect his corpse. He knew which mortuary he would be taken to, who would remove his clothing from his body and who would wash his body with alcohol solution taken from which container; who would lay him out on the dissecting table. He knew who would take which knife and who would make incisions here and here and here, and who would then peel the flesh from his face and chest. A case of a man in the wrong job if ever there was one, so Sussock had always thought. Mr Duffy, all those years ago and now doubtless long deceased, would have made a contented gardener or postman or baker, but not a mortuary assistant. Sussock could never imagine the work of a mortuary assistant would reach Dr Reynolds's usual assistant like the work had reached Mr Duffy. Again, Sussock was pleased that that man was not present this Sunday afternoon.

'Well, we are presented with a corpse.' Reynolds slid a surgical-gloved hand into the pocket of his smock and switched on the tape-recorder. He spoke in a normal voice,

22

with the small microphone in the lapel of his smock recording his voice without his having to direct it sideways to the microphone. 'And, as on all such occasions, we will attempt to determine the cause of death. The date is March 31st, the deceased, a male, is . . .' Reynolds glanced at Sussock. Sussock shook his head. 'ID to be confirmed,' continued Reynolds, though Sussock knew that a Social Security card found in the pocket of the deceased's jeans giving the name of one Edward Wroe and an address in Kelvinbridge seemed to be a promising lead.

'Initially, I intend to determine the approximate time of death and then the cause.' Reynolds lifted one arm of the corpse and let it fall on the table. He did the same with one spindly leg. He then placed his hand behind the neck of the deceased and lifted it up just an inch or two off the table. Sussock saw that the pathologist had to apply considerably greater strength to do this than it had required to lift the limbs. The neck, in contrast to the limbs, seemed stiff and rigidly attached to the shoulders. It did not hinge forward, but rather, when Reynolds lifted the neck, the upper torso also lifted from the table.

'Inconsistency in the extent of rigor is noted,' said Reynolds and then, in an aside to Sussock, 'Dr Chan's humble observation was quite accurate.'

'Indeed,' said Sussock.

'Neck and shoulder muscles reveal rigor mortis as would be expected with noted rectal temperature of one degree Celsius. The limbs remain supple.' The silver-haired pathologist smiled at Sussock. 'That's not a mystery at all,' he said, 'I know what the answer is. Mind you, it's going to prove to be a bit of a poser for you chaps.'

'What happened, sir?' Sussock asked, his voice echoing in the spartan room.

'All in good time, Sergeant. All in good time.' Reynolds surveyed the body. 'There are a number of incised wounds and penetrating wounds about the chest, some very superficial, but two stab wounds seem to have penetrated, one to the aorta, I would think, judging by its location, which probably would have been the fatal wound, and a second to the upper shoulder; this last seems to have penetrated the artery and would have been fatal within minutes had the first not been fatal within seconds.' He paused again and turned to Sussock. 'I didn't notice a great deal of blood at the apparent locus of the offence. Did you, Sergeant? There is no reference to blood in my notes.'

'There was none, sir,' said Sussock. 'I made a special point of checking my own notes before attending here. I thought it strange that, given the amount of blood on the clothing, there should be little, in fact no blood, on the walls or the cobbles.'

'It doesn't surprise me that you said that, Sergeant.' Reynolds laid his hands on the side of the dissecting table. 'You see, the indication is that the body was moved after death and deposited in the location where it was subsequently found.'

'Oh.' Sussock involuntarily stepped one pace forward.

'Well, yes, you see, with the body temperature as low as it is, we usually divide 99 by 1.5 to arrive at an indication of number of hours dead, 99 being the degrees Fahrenheit of the body when alive and 1.5 the number of degrees per hour that the body will lose temperature, at room temperature. Now, given the actual body temperature as noted, I would expect to find that rigor had already set in and was well established. I do in fact find rigor in the neck, but, as you perhaps saw, there is suppleness in the limbs.' Reynolds stroked his chin. 'The answer to the puzzle is that the body was murdered elsewhere and lay elsewhere during which time rigor set in, then the body was moved and, in doing so, the rigor was "broken", as we say. You see, once a limb which is stiff with rigor has been forced to move, a knee is forced to bend, for example, then the rigor will not re-establish itself and the joint will remain pliable.'

'So,' said Sussock, 'the body lay at another location for some time after death and then the murderer—'

'Or an accomplice, Sergeant. Keep your options open.'

'—or an accomplice moved the body, forcing the limbs to bend in doing so.'

'Yes.' Reynolds nodded. 'That's it; and he did that about

24

twelve hours after death. It would need that time to allow
rigor to set in to the extent that it has set in around his neck,
which has not been "broken" in that sense.'

'I see, sir.' Sussock felt awkward. 'Why would the murderer want to move the limbs, what advantage is there?'
Even though Sussock had pondered the question aloud,
more to himself than to Reynolds, Reynolds picked it up.

'The only reason could be to compress the body, Sergeant,
to bend the knees up to the chest, for example. Let's see,
shall we?' Reynolds took the right leg behind the knee and
moved it up to the man's chest. 'Yes, that's it.' He let the
leg down again. 'You see, both the knee and the hip moved
easily. The body was folded up to conceal it, probably in a
sack or a chest, for example.'

'Yes, of course.'

'But in this case the body hadn't been folded upon death,
otherwise rigor would have set in while it was in the folded
position.'

'In fact, what you're saying, sir, is that the body stiffened
in a prone position, it was "broken" and concealed and
transported to the locus where it was found, with the joints
once again elastic.'

'Yes, giving the immediate impression that rigor had just
begun to set in, but it didn't fool the sharp eyes of your
police surgeon. Good man is Chan; on the ball. So in fact,
when the body was found, the rigor was about twelve hours
old. Perhaps you'd like to help me?'

'Sir?' Sussock stepped forward.

'If you'd take his feet . . .'

Sussock did so. Cold and clammy.

'After three, anti-clockwise . . .'

With the posterior aspect upwards, the body looked painfully thin and wasted.

'Poor skin,' said Reynolds. 'I mean, for his age. It
wouldn't surprise me if he was verging on the brink of
scurvy.'

'Really?' Sussock was surprised. 'I thought that went out
with the wooden sailing ships?'

'Not a bit of it. If you live on a diet of beer and tinned

beans, especially a lot of the former, and have no fresh fruit or vegetables or fresh meat, then you'll get scurvy. It's caused by a poor diet, as is rickets, which even today is not uncommon in Asian children because they don't get the nutrients from the sun here in the West and the typical diet of an Asian family doesn't compensate for that loss. But to address ourselves to the matter in hand: you see the reddening of the shoulder-blades, the lumbar region and the buttocks? Also, there's a little reddening at the heel of each foot?'

Sussock noted the said reddening.

'That is what we call hypostasis. We are particularly lucky that our friend is a thin person, because hypostasis is often difficult to detect. What it is, simply, is blood which has drained down the body according to gravitational pull and has collected at the point or points where the body is in contact with the surface on which it is resting.'

'So if the body was laying face down, on its front, then hypostasis would be noticed on the chest?'

'Exactly, but in this case, the reddening is on the posterior aspect.'

'So, the body was left lying on its back?'

'That's it.'

'For twelve hours, until rigor had set in?'

'That's it.'

'Then it was moved, the rigor was broken to facilitate transport or for concealment, and it was then dumped where it was found.'

'That's it. Breaking the rigor wouldn't have thrown me off the scent, so I think that you can assume that the breaking was done for logistical reasons rather than to lay a false scent, if you see what I mean?'

'I see, sir.'

'I think you'll find a considerable amount of blood at the actual locus, because the hypostasis in this incident is faint, it would be significantly darker had most or all of the eight pints remained in the body, especially in such an emaciated body.'

'Could you indicate the probable time of death, sir?'

Sussock pressed Reynolds. 'In the light of this evidence?'

Reynolds pondered. 'Rigor can set in rapidly or be delayed. A person who dies in his sleep in a warm bed in a warm room will have their rigor delayed. A person whose death is associated with fear, or activity, will have a rapid onset of rigor. This poor chap was stabbed to death from the front; he would have been in fear of his life; there's a small laceration to the palm of his right hand, indicating that he's right-handed and he tried to grab the blade, or use his hands to shield his torso. He knew what was happening to him and his last waking moments would have been moments of terror. His adrenalin would have been pumping, his heart racing . . . In his case, rigor would have set in rapidly, within twelve hours. Then he lay face up, and rigor established itself . . . It's really hard to say, Sergeant.'

'Even a reasoned and educated guess at this stage would be of great assistance, sir.'

'Well, say within twenty-four hours as of now. The body was located at eight a.m. today, death may have occurred nineteen or twenty hours before that.'

'Midday, yesterday, sir?' Sussock pressed.

'That sort of time scale, within a four-hour "envelope" of midday yesterday. Not before ten a.m., probably not later than two or three p.m. Does that help?'

Sussock said that it did and it didn't. As they rotated the corpse of the man believed to be one Edward Wroe anti-clockwise after three, so that once again his lifeless face looked up towards the filament bulbs and the starched towel was once again draped over his private parts, Reynolds asked Sussock what he meant.

'Only that I had thought it to be another Saturday-night knifing. One ned cooling another, when both deep in the drink.'

'I know the sort of thing,' said Reynolds.

'So now it seems we can discount that,' said Sussock. 'Solve one riddle and pursue another. That's what it feels like. You see, what I can't understand is, if someone is going to take the trouble of breaking a stiff's rigor, why also take the risk of bringing it into the town and leaving it where it will be rapidly found? I would have thought it would be more sensible to take it out to Fenwick Moor and dowse it with petrol and incinerate it. That would really cause us problems.'

'Not insurmountable problems,' said Reynolds sharply, 'but I take your point. I think you said that you found the murder weapon?'

'We—well, I found a knife, sir. It's at the Forensic Laboratory at present.'

'Can you describe it?'

'Common or garden five-inch thin-bladed kitchen knife, wooden handle. I've got one in my house and I dare say you have one in yours. It was found close to the body, heavily bloodstained.'

'Well, it's certainly the sort of weapon that would cause injuries like this, there is the characteristic "fish-tailing" of the stab wounds typical of injuries caused by a thin blade, and five inches is easily sufficient to reach the aorta; it would have penetrated the shoulder artery with four inches to spare. Send it over and I'll test it as I promised I would.' Reynolds took a short-bladed instrument from the instrument trolley. 'I'll scrape under his fingernails and see what tales they tell, then I'll open up his stomach and see what he had for his last meal in life and when he had it. Will you stay?'

Sussock said he thought perhaps not, if the good doctor didn't mind. Perhaps the results could be phoned in.

He left the mortuary of the Glasgow Royal Infirmary, walking down the cream-painted corridor with pipes on the ceiling and doors off to the left and right, some with yellow radiation warning signs on them. He walked up the wide staircase to the ground floor and left by the main doorway. He walked across the car park with the magnificent façade of the building behind him and left the hospital proper via the casualty department. At that moment the casualty department was enjoying a lull, the trolleys were empty, the examination booths had their curtains drawn open. A doctor, young-looking, childishly young to Sussock's eyes, sat on a trolley writing up a file. Two nurses stood chatting to each other; in the reception cubicle someone laughed at a joke. It was the calm before the storm. Even on a Sunday, from 10.0 p.m. onwards, the casualty department at the GRI would be crowded with bloodily damaged people nursing wounds, many smelling of alcohol, and grey cardboard vomit-bowls and rolls of tissue would litter the floor; new graffiti would be added to the walls. Relatives would have to be comforted, others would burst into tears with relief.

Sussock walked through the automatic doors and left the hospital through the ambulance bay and walked to where he had left his car. The empty Sunday-afternoon streets allowed him a smooth drive through the city, past the new residential buildings of Strathclyde University, over the Queen Street Station railway bridge, where a down-and-out was scrubbing the cast-iron railings with a toothbrush. Sussock drove along Bath Street up to the summit, crossing a series of major roads that was the grid system of Glasgow Town, driving between imposing lines of Victorian buildings. He drove down the further side of Bath Street towards Charing Cross where the motorway drives a trench through the city. He turned off the thoroughfare and into the car park at the rear of the police station at Charing Cross. Sussock entered the building in a bustling flurry of an open raincoat and wide, baggy trousers, holding a battered hat in one hand, pushing doors open with the other. The phone on his desk rang just at the instant that he tossed his hat on to the peg at the top of the coat-stand.

'Sussock,' he said, standing at his desk, still with his raincoat hanging from his shoulders.

'Switchboard, sir,' said a young man's voice, and a ltitle nervous too, thought Sussock. 'Dr Kay, Forensic Laboratory, phoned when you were out. She requested you phone her back. She said that she'd be in the laboratory until fourteen-thirty.'

'There was no message in my pigeonhole.'

'I had no time to put it in, sir. Then I was told that you had entered the building.'

'Not good enough, laddie, not good enough at all. It's a

29

vital message. Make time. Ask someone to do it for you. Who are you?'

'PC Chandler, sir.'

'New here?'

'Yes, sir, straight from Training College.'

'Learn from this incident, Chandler.'

'Yes, sir.'

Sussock put the phone down. He glanced at the digital clock on his office wall. 14.25. He took his coat off and hung it from the peg beneath his hat. It was a battered, shapeless coat and he had long since given up hanging it from a hanger. These days it drooped like a sack from the peg. He returned to his desk and phoned Jean Kay, Ph.D. at the Forensic Laboratory.

'Speaking,' said Dr Kay, after a pause and after the line had clicked twice. She had a soft voice, authoritative without being overbearing.

'DS Sussock,' said Sussock, 'P Division. Returning your call.'

'Oh yes. The clothing and the knife. Well, the knife is a promising source of information. Blood on the knife matches the blood group of the deceased. A positive, as given by telephone from the GRI. A Dr Reynolds, I believe?'

'That's correct, madam,' said Sussock. 'In fact, I've just come from Dr Reynolds's theatre in the GRI.'

'I see. Well, as I said, the blood group clearly matches up. There are a number of fudged fingerprints on the blade and the handle of the knife, but one very clear print on the handle. We have photographed it and I have laid the knife on one side in a sealed container should you wish your forensic assistant to lift the latent. We'll get the report to you by courier later this afternoon.'

'Thank you, madam,' said Sussock crisply.

'I have to point out what may be strange, and equally may have a simple explanation, and that is that the print on the handle, the one clear print on the knife, is reverse to the blade. What I mean by that is that the person who left the print on the handle was at the time holding the knife as he would if he were holding the blade towards him, not away from him as he would have been if he was using the knife as a weapon. The smudged prints on the handle and the blade indicate that the knife at some point was held in the conventional manner, that is to say the manner which it would have been held if it was to be used as a weapon, with the blade pointing away from the holder. Similarly, though your forensic assistant may confirm this, it seems to me that the gloved hand, the one which left the smudges, the gloved hand was not the hand which left the latent. The gloved hand was much bigger and heavier. I'll make reference to it in my report.'

Again Sussock said, 'Thank you, madam.' He relaxed in his chair and then leaned backwards, as he found that he tended to do when speaking with a certain professional expertise. 'Weapons like that knife are passed from ned to ned, sold for the price of a pint of lager. It's not surprising that there are a number of different prints on it.'

'I see,' said Dr Kay, receptive to Sussock's knowledge. 'How does that explain the reverse print on the handle? To hold the blade like that would imply that the assailant was standing beside or even in front of his victim.'

'Knives are often concealed inside jacket sleeves,' said Sussock, 'reverse way up, either in the sleeve opposite to the hand which holds the knife so the person reaches across and slides the knife out, or sometimes it's held in the sleeve of the hand which holds the knife, so that the knife drops handle first into the person's palm and is then swivelled in the fingers.'

'I see,' Dr Kay replied slowly. 'That would certainly seem to account for the position of the thumb print and the series of smudged prints. How interesting.'

'Nothing on the clothing, madam?'

'Dirty, cheap, thin; he would have suffered from the cold if this was all he was wearing at this time of year. I've found traces of motor oil in the denim, as if he had lain face up in a pool of oil. All I can tell you at the present is that it's oil with grit and metal filings . . .'

'An industrial site?'

'I'd say the floor of a garage,' said Dr Kay. 'I'll do more

31

tests and try to pin down the type of oil, grit and metal, but what I can tell you as of now is that it's a recent impregnation. There is no evidence of previous prolonged or regular contact; the site of impregnation is too localized. It's all embedded in the rear of the clothing, nothing similar on the front. It is not as though they are his working clothes.'

'I see.' Sussock pinned the phone between his ear and his shoulder while he scribbled notes on his pad. 'How recent, can you say, madam?'

'The oil is still fluid. It's still sticky to the touch. The simple tests are the most accurate. Within twenty-four hours.'

'Interesting. The pathologist—'

'Dr Reynolds?'

'Yes. He is of the opinion that the attack itself took place elsewhere to the locus at which the body was found.'

'Well, that would not be out of the question, not at all at odds with my findings to date. That is to say that it seems that the young man was attacked and murdered in a garage or on an industrial site and then taken to the alley where I am led to believe that he was found. Yes, I have discovered nothing to indicate that he was murdered where he was found.'

'The pathologist believes that he was allowed to lie where he was murdered and then moved some hours later. There is apparently evidence that the rigor has been "broken", as he said.'

'I know what he means, and in point of fact that would fit in entirely with the degree of impregnation of the oil. The body lay on a dirty, oily surface long enough for the jacket and jeans and shirt to soak up oil and become extensively impregnated. As I said, he seems to have lain face up because there is no indication of oil impregnation on the front of his clothing.'

'Again,' said Sussock, 'Dr Reynolds said that the body lay face up for some time, because what blood remained in the body settled on the shoulder-blades and the lumbar regions.'

32

'Ties in nicely,' said Dr Kay. 'Ties in very neatly indeed. Do you know who he is?'

'Well, that,' said Sussock, 'is the next difficult task.'

'Mrs Wroe?' Elka Willems glanced at the woman, ashen-faced, matted hair, who blinked empty-headedly at her. Elka Willems thought that the woman didn't seem at all surprised that a female police officer should be knocking at her door. 'Mrs Wroe!' said Elka Willems with a little more insistence.

This time the woman nodded between blinks.

'Perhaps I can come inside?' Elka Willems pressed. The close was a public place, she was aware of two people, perhaps three, standing above her beyond the turn of the stair. The wind blew off the Clyde whose wide, choppy waters lay behind her as she approached the drab 1930's low-rise tenement development. The smell of Greenock filled her nostrils. Not being a native of Glasgow or its environs, she had long thought that the musty smell of Greenock emanated from the shipyards and it was not until recently that she had found that the smell which hung heavy in the air over the town was in fact coming from the glue factory where the carcases of animals were being boiled down into fluid. As she climbed the chipped, cracked concrete steps with long, litter-strewn grass at either side of her, she noticed the face at the first-floor landing turn excitedly at the sight of her uniform and then retreat into the gloom. She entered the close, littered with sweet wrappers, the walls filled with sectarian graffiti. The first door, bottom left, had WROE written on the green paint with a black dry-marker pen. Elka Willems rapped the door-knocker and heard the studied silence of two or three people waiting beyond the turn of the stair, curious as to the reason for her call- ing. When at last the door opened and the small woman blinked at her out of a darkened, damp-smelling hallway, Elka Willems said, 'Mrs Wroe, perhaps I can come inside?'

The woman kept on blinking; Elka Willems looked into dark, small, tortured eyes. Then the woman turned and walked down a dim narrow corridor with gift shop decorations nailed to the wall. Elka Willems interpreted the woman's act as in invitation to enter.

The front room of the house was untidy and cluttered, making a small space seem even smaller. A dog jumped up at Elka Willems as she entered, jumping up excitedly, running round her, tail wagging, but to her surprise it made no attempt to bark.

'He's my only companion.' The woman spoke for the first time. She had a tired, exhausted voice, the voice of someone who had been beaten by life. A person who is 'hope extinct'. 'He just doesn't bark. Never has. Jodie, that's his name.'

Elka Willems looked about her. The room seemed to be decorated with Christian ornaments and prints. A television sat in the corner. The curtains were drawn shut, yet it was still only late afternoon. The electric light shone and the gas fire was full on.

'I'm in the army,' said the woman in a flat voice, but Elka Willems thought that she detected just a hint of pride.

'I'm sorry?'

'I'm in the army.' She nodded to an engraving of Christ with birds flocking about him. It hung above the small mantelpiece. 'The Salvation Army.'

'I see,' said Elka Willems. 'Very good. Well, I'm afraid that I may have some bad news for you, Mrs Wroe.'

'I'm paying five pounds a week towards my uniform.' Mrs Wroe sank into an armchair which was overfull with cushions of ill-matching colours. 'Money's tight. I'm on social security. Last week I had three pounds left at the end of the week and this week I've just got a pound to do me until Tuesday when I cash my order book. I've got some tins on the shelf, though.'

'You have a son, Eddie? Edward, I presume?'

'I haven't seen Eddie for a year.'

'Mrs Wroe, Eddie . . . I'm afraid Eddie was killed this morning.'

No reaction.

'We believe that it may be Eddie.' Elka Willems found her voice hardening with impatience at the woman's lack of perceptible personality. 'He had a wallet . . . we found a wallet, a small plastic holder in the back pocket of his jeans. There was no money but he did have the good sense to keep a note of his next of kin in case of an accident. The address given was your address, Mrs Wroe, and a social security card in the wallet gave the name "Eddie Wroe".'

'What? Eddie?' She looked into the flames of the gas fire for a second, for two, for ten, as if becoming mesmerized.

'Mrs Wroe! Mrs Wroe, I'll need to ask you to accompany me. We have to visit the mortuary in Glasgow.'

'In Glasgow! I'm to be at the Chapel for six p.m. I've to do the flowers this month.'

'I'll get you back on time. Where's your coat? It's windy outside.'

Throughout the journey to Glasgow, Mrs Wroe sat in the front seat of the car, smelling strongly of damp, with a cheap plastic handbag perched on her lap, like a timid child. She stared blankly at the road ahead of her, saying nothing and, thought Elka Willems, probably noticing or seeing nothing either.

In the basement of the Royal Infirmary, Dr Reynolds, who had remained to write up his report of the post-mortem on the man believed to be Edward Wroe, transcribing from his taped commentary, embellishing as he did so, escorted Elka Willems and the fragile, short-stepping, right-hand-handbag-clutching Mrs Wroe into the chilled and chilling room where banks of steel drawers lined the wall. With a sobriety and seriousness of manner and with a gentle yet purposeful movement, he slid open one of the drawers and parted the sheet to reveal the finely made features of the young person believed to be Edward Wroe.

Elka Willems noted with an experienced eye that the deceased had facial features known as 'pixie features', smaller than normal, pointed nose, sunken eyes, slightly elongated ears. The features would have been more marked in childhood and were symptomatic of foetal alcohol syndrome. If this timid, shuffling woman was the deceased's mother, reflected Elka Willems, then twenty years ago she wouldn't have been timid and shuffling. She would have been a serious bevvy merchant, heavily into the super lagers and cigarettes and doing both to excess from the beginning to the end of pregnancy, and so would attest to the quality of the childhood of the occupant of the drawer.

The frightened and fragile Mrs Wroe nodded and said, 'Aye, that is him, that's our Eddie.'

Dr Reynolds re-covered the face with the sheet and slid the body of Edward Wroe back into the wall with a solid clunk.

'We have some personal effects, but we have to retain them, for the time being at least,' said Elka Willems solemnly. 'We'll release them as soon as we can. I take it that you are the next of kin, as Eddie indicated?'

'Aye.' Uninterestedly.

The woman shuffled behind Elka Willems as they made their way out of the Glasgow Royal, following the tall WPC with the striking Nordic looks at a snail's pace as they left the bowels of the hospital, making their way by corridor and stair to the blustery, darkening Glasgow late March Sunday evening.

'It's not a stupid question,' said Elka Willems, attempting to provoke some reaction from the woman who had just seen her son in a mortuary drawer and who was anxious to get back to Greenock to arrange the flowers in the Chapel. 'The note giving your name and address could have been in his wallet for some time, during which time he might have married, in which case . . .'

'He didn't marry,' said Mrs Wroe, with a sharpness, curtness, which surprised Elka Willems and made her think, somewhat cynically, she conceded, that there might be life after death after all. Elka Willems wondered what had happened to Mrs Wroe in the last twenty years that the spirit of a heavy drinker had been battered out of her, leaving just an empty shell with the occasional propensity towards curtness, and then only if pushed far enough.

'What,' she asked, 'was Eddie doing for the last twelve months?'

'Living in the city,' she said. 'He didn't tell me much. He never asked me for money, he didn't send me any either, even when he knew I was in the Army and paying five pounds a week for my uniform, and that had to come out of my benefit.'

'What about Eddie's father, would he know?'

'I never knew which one was Eddie's father,' she said with disarming honesty.

'I see.'

'Do you think I'll be back for six o'clock?'

Elka Willems glanced at her watch. 17.10. 'Yes,' she said, 'I should think so.'

CHAPTER 3

Sunday, 18.30–Monday 02.30 hours

Richard King thought that Ray Sussock looked pleased with himself. As well he might, he added as an afterthought. King had to concede that it was neat, very neat. Victim identified, murder weapon found, prints lifted, which in the event proved to be those of a known felon, one Shane Dodemaide. Not only was Dodemaide a known felon but he was a known felon with convictions for violence, and not only that, but he was a known felon who was known to the deceased.

They shared a common address.

King, chubby, bearded, twenty-five years of age, sat in front of Sussock's desk and nodded appreciatively. Yes, he had to concede that it was very, very neat.

'Murders are always grubby.' Sussock spoke with an air of self-satisfied authority. Outside rain fell, splattering on the office window; if either man looked sideways towards the window he would see his reflection and beyond that the lights of the city in the early evening darkness. 'I dare say you've found that out for yourself by now, Richard. Far more often than not, they are usually wrapped up in a matter of hours, days at the outside. As in this case.'

'Certainly seems clear-cut.' King glanced over Sussock's notes still in legible longhand awaiting typing. 'What's the next step?'

'Go and bring in Mr Dodemaide.' Sussock leaned back in his chair, causing it to creak. 'Fondle his collar, ask him what he knows about the murder of Mr Eddie Wroe.'

'Has the deceased been positively identified?' King asked, sensing Sussock to be savouring every moment of his success.

'Waiting for Elka Willems to come back to me. Ought not to be too long now.' He glanced at the black telephone on his desk. 'We'll wait for her to return or phone in with the result and then we'll go and lift Mr Dodemaide.'

'I presume that we'd still pick him up anyway, Sarge? I mean, his prints being on the murder weapon.'

'Oh yes, certainly, I'd just like to make sure that we are charging him with the murder of Eddie Wroe and not the murder of another as yet unidentified person. But it has to be Wroe—just look at the list of p.c.'s we got from Scottish Criminal Records at Pitt Street and the addresses thereon. Both live at the same address in Belmont Street in Kelvin-bridge, both have p.c.'s for robbery, and Dodemaide went down for a wee stretch for assault to severe injury. Eddie Wroe was twenty years of age, Dodemaide is twenty-one, both have convictions going back to when they were fifteen, all petty stuff, opening lockfast premises right through to possession of narcotics, given a modest fine for that.'

'Says a lot,' said King. 'I mean, if they were given a modest fine for possession, it means that they're addicts and the amount in question was minute. Any larger an amount and the slightest suggestion of dealing and they would both have gone down for a few years.' King looked sideways at his reflection and thought that his beard needed trimming. 'Just as you said, Sarge. What do you think happened—one smack-head knifes another in a petty argument?'

'I'm thinking along those lines. I know what their address is going to be like; young wasted bodies lying about, bucket full of vomit in the centre of the room, a streak of blood up

38

the wall where one smack-head has punctured an artery. Tread carefully, Richard.'

'Am I doing it?' King smiled.

'Well, you are the back shift for your sins and I am handing over a neat "package".' Sussock raised an eyebrow. 'I'll hang on until WPC Willems feeds back, just to satisfy myself that the victim has been properly identified, and I'll leave it from then on in your most capable hands. Obviously, I'd like to stay to see it to the end, but it appears to be straightforward enough.'

'Well, he's certainly got some explaining to do,' King conceded, closing the file and placing it on Sussock's desk.

'He hasn't half,' said Sussock. 'He hasn't half.'

It was a large room, a darkly stained, large, heavy door at one end, and, at the other, a bay window of tall sheets of glass. The floor was covered in an Axminster carpet. At either side of the room shelves of books reached from floor to ceiling. A large rectangular table stood in the centre. There was a bowl of flowers on the table. A man sat at the table. He was powerfully built, broad chested, thick muscular arms, a bald head with a band of silver hair running from above each ear round the back of his head. He was cleaning the barrel of a revolver. A woman stood beside him. She was short of stature, short hair, plainly cut, like a girl from an orphanage; she wore a floral patterned skirt, a white lace blouse. She wrung her hands and closed her eyes as if close to weeping. 'Please!' she said.

'No.' The man didn't look at her as he pulled the cloth through the barrel of the revolver.

'You haven't seen her, you don't know how bad she is, a doctor . . .'

'There'll be no doctors.' The man spoke slowly, quietly, softly, menacingly. There was no hint of compromise. 'We've been through this before. I'm not prepared to go through it again.'

'You can't say that when you haven't seen her . . . or heard her, the noise she makes . . . she's like a woman possessed.'

'It'll pass. In a few days it will have passed. It's hysteria and nothing more.'

'Hysteria! She's doubled up, writhing on the floor. She's making sounds from deep inside her throat and that's only because she keeps her teeth gritted so she won't scream with the agony.'

The man laid the gun down on the velvet cloth which covered the old table and looked up at the woman. He thought her pathetic. He remembered her twenty years ago when they were still newly lovers, then she had had some spark, some vitality, some personality. But not now, now she was a wimpish timid creature, without any backbone, now she would cower when he looked at her. She was a great disappointment to him. It was too late to divorce now and it would look bad; he would keep her at home out of harm's way. Thank the Lord, he thought, thank the Lord that they had had but the one child. A mother like this creature was not a thing any man could wish on any child. One child to resent him was enough, to resent him for providing it with such a weak mother. Heavens, she was more like a little sister to Veronica than she was like a mother. Even from the earliest days, she would give in to the child.

'Don't look at me like that, David,' she whimpered, interrupting his thoughts. 'I don't like it when you look at me like that. Your eyes are so steely cold, it upsets me. I never know what you are thinking, but it doesn't look pleasant. Can't you have good thoughts about me and Veronica? I try; I put some fresh flowers on your table . . .'

'I noticed,' the man growled as he laid the gun down and picked up another identical weapon.

'Veronica . . .'

'No.'

'David . . .'

'There'll be no doctors. I want no outside help. We don't need it. She doesn't need it. That is final. It'll do her good, it's called cold caring. If a man comes home drunk and falls flat on his face, you leave him there so he wakes up confronted by his own drink problem; you don't clean him up and put him to bed so he wakes up in clean sheets. That just helps him to avoid the problem. Veronica got herself into this mess. She'll have to get herself out of it. She'll think twice before doing it again.'

'I'll need to stay with her tonight and tomorrow, and as long as it takes.'

'No.'

'I must.'

'No, it'll make her worse! She'll just play up to your attention. What you are seeing is just hysterical nonsense.'

'It isn't, sir . . .'

The man's jaw dropped. My God, that just took the cake . . . that just took the cake. Now she was calling him, her husband, 'sir'. No wonder Veronica was so hysterical. If this was his weak-willed mother, he'd be hysterical as well.

'It's no worse than 'flu.'

'Are you a doctor now?'

A bit of fight—not bad—if he pushed her enough, she might even stamp her foot.

'No, I'm not, and you know fine well that I'm not. I'm a lawyer and a damn good one and you've done well out of my success, not that you're the slightest bit grateful. Perhaps you ought to have married a primary school teacher and had a new second-hand car once every five years and a foreign holiday every ten years. Maybe then . . .'

The woman began to weep.

'Just get out. Go back to your snivelling daughter . . . but I want you in the house tonight, beside me, in my bed, between me and the wall, where you belong.'

The woman nodded her head vigorously and then scurried out of the room with quick, apologetic little steps.

Elka Willems drove into the rear car park of P Division police station. She entered the building and went upstairs to the CID corridor. She tapped on Sussock's door and entered his office. Sussock sat at his desk, Richard King sat in front of it.

'Just handing over the Eddie Wroe case,' said Sussock, 'among a few other things.' He smiled at her. 'I presume it is Edward Wroe?'

41

'Positive ID, Sarge,' said Willems, who still managed to be stunningly attractive in the unflattering serge uniform of a WPC. She addressed both Sussock and King, who had turned in his chair to face her. 'Mrs Wroe identified the deceased as that of her son.'

'Upset?'

'Not very.' Elka Willems remained on the threshold of Sussock's office. 'She seemed more upset at the prospect of getting back too late to do the flowers at the Citadel.'

'The Citadel?'

'She's in the Salvation Army. Just enlisted, I think, because she's paying off her uniform at a fiver a week. But that's by the way. The deceased is Eddie Wroe, late of Greenock.'

Richard King turned back to face Sussock and Elka Willems took the opportunity to wink at Sussock before closing the door behind her.

'Well, so it's over to you, Richard.' Sussock stood and reached for his seat. 'Be very careful how you go. Don't cut yourself on anything in a druggie's place of residence.'

Wroe and Dodemaide's place of residence was at the bottom of Belmont Street, Kelvinbridge, G12. Belmont Street thrust at ninety degrees from the traffic lights and trendy shops and pubs and nite-spots on Great Western Road, rising up to the bridge over the Kelvin where a few weeks previously two thugs had suspended a young man over the parapet, threatening to drop him sixty feet into the freezing waters below because he was unable to give them the cigarettes they demanded. The houses at the bottom of Belmont Street were solid sandstone terraced property, each on three levels, fabulous homes in their heyday, but now in a state of disrepair, some empty, shored up with timbers, others boarded up with corrugated iron which was easily torn down by the city's down-and-outs, ready and convenient for all amenities: 'skippering' premises. On one property, the entire rear wall had recently fallen, hingeing backwards from the ground like a solid expanse of brick, crashing down with some good fortune, on to empty waste ground. Its collapse exposed rough areas in the ground floor and the first and second floors, odd sticks of furniture, mattresses on the floor, wallpaper peeling from the walls. The City wanted to demolish the houses and renovate the area for redevelopment; pressure groups wanted the houses themselves to be renovated, seeing them as part of the city's rich Victorian architectural heritage.

It was dark and drizzling steadily when King turned his car right, off Great Western Road and into Belmont Street, followed by a van containing two uniformed officers. He pulled to a halt outside the address given on Eddie Wroe's social security card, the same address given on the list of p.c.'s held by SCRO on both the deceased and Shane Dodemaide. King looked at the house. Grey paint faded over the chipped stonework. The building was mostly in darkness. A light shone from an upper window. He checked his watch: 23.40.

It had been a routine back shift, warrants served, paperwork done, details of thefts taken, suspicious persons being reported by members of the public and responded to with some success: a car with three youths sitting outside a house known to be empty and reported by a sharp-eyed member of the public turned out to be three youths wanted in connection with housebreaking offences. A visit to their homes revealed their bedrooms to be Aladdin's caves of identifiable stolen goods, watches, clocks, video recorders, credit cards, fur coats and sheepskin jackets. That, King had found, was often the way of it, one phone-call can crack a case, as in this instance; an entire string of housebreakings had been wrapped up by a single phone-call. Three ashen-faced youths of good and somewhat indulged middle-class homes sat in the detention rooms. They had lawyers provided by devastated parents, but the case against each was concrete and they were looking at two to three years' youth custody, during which time they would be banged up for twenty-three hours a day with some of the toughest, hardest and most twisted neds in Scotland.

Shane Dodemaide, King reasoned, had better be left until later in the shift. The communication network among the drug-abusers had always astounded King with its speed and efficiency and clarity of transmission of information. If he called too early and Dodemaide wasn't in, then wherever he was, he'd hear within thirty minutes that the law was hunting him and he'd go to ground. Unless, King reasoned, unless he heard that the law was on his trail, then he wouldn't be going anywhere; best to leave it, he thought, best to leave it until there's half a chance of catching him at home. Twenty minutes to midnight seemed to him to be as good a time as any.

King got out of the car and put his collar up against the rain. He walked up to the front door of the house and, as he approached the building, smelled the musty smell of damp emanating from the sandstone. The two constables, in capes, followed him. He walked up the slippery uneven flagstones to the front door and pressed the doorbell. Not a sound. He rapped on the door twice and heard the sound echoing inside the building.

He stood in the rain and looked at the constables. He raised his eyebrows, but they remained stone-faced. Eventually, a thin, squeaky, female voice called from within, 'Who is it?'

King didn't reply. Again the voice said, 'Who is it?'

King knocked on the door twice.

Silence from within the building.

A car passed behind them, going up Belmont Street, its tyres hissing on the wet surface of the road.

Again the voice said, 'Who is it?' The voice was closer than before, maybe one flight up. King expected one of the windows above them to slide open and a head peer out, but the occupants of the house did not take that precaution, or couldn't—most likely the window-frames had warped and rotted, jamming them shut.

'Who is it?' This time she was just behind the door.

'Police,' said King.

'Polis! Polis!' The woman screamed and seemed to fly into a panic.

King stepped aside. 'Punt it in.'

The two officers put their shoulders to the door. It gave easily and the cops entered the building in time to see a

44

skinny girl in blue jeans leaping up the stairs two at a time, still shouting, 'Polis! Polis!' One of the uniformed officers ran after her and caught her easily. In the house doors were slammed shut, there was the sound of furniture being dragged across the floors and placed against the doors. Someone switched the hall light off.

King groped for a switch and turned it back on. It stayed on.

A male voice yelled, 'Drug Squad. It's a bust!' Upstairs a window smashed.

King climbed the stairs. On the first-floor landing one officer held the skinny girl in blue jeans. She was a waif, pale and drawn. She looked to be about thirteen.

'How old are you?' he asked as he approached the girl.

'Seventeen.'

'What's your name?'

'Sadie Kelly.' She had a soft Irish accent.

'And you're seventeen.'

'Aye.'

'Well, you don't look it, Sadie Kelly, so we'll take you in until we can check it out.'

The girl struggled violently.

'We're looking for Shane Dodemaide,' said King. Sadie Kelly glared at him.

'Look, Sadie Kelly,' King said softly, 'it works like this. If you are seventeen and there's no outstanding warrants out on you, then you can leave the police station. We are not DS, so we're not going to search your room. But if you don't help us, we'll prefer charges like resisting arrest, obstructing the police, wasting police time and anything else that we can think of. And if we do that, we'll detain you in custody until your trial, because this is a squat. We can't and won't recognize it as an address. So—where is Shane Dodemaide?'

'That room there.' She indicated the door immediately on King's right.

'Couldn't be more convenient,' said King.

He knocked on the door. From within came the sound of someone murmuring. King was amused that someone could

45

sleep through the recent commotion, even when there were voices raised outside his very door.

'Who is it?' said a sleepy voice.

'Shane Dodemaide?'

'Aye.'

'Police. Open up.'

The door clicked open. A pale youth in blue jeans stood blinking in the doorway and King wondered if all the pale and emaciated waifs in the city lived in this house.

Dodemaide had an odd face and King reproached himself for being cynical, trying as he was to live up to the high-minded ideals of his wonderful Quaker wife. None the less, he couldn't help but be struck by Dodemaide's features. The boy had a sharply receding forehead which in profile would have run in a continuous line to a pointed nose. He had a small mouth, below which was a receding, barely perceptible chin. He had loud, centrally parted ginger hair and a ginger moustache which extended widely at either side of his face. To King he looked not unlike a caricature of a rat.

'Am I under arrest again?' he said sleepily.

'Yes.'

'I choose to remain silent. What are you going to pin on me this time—breach of the peace? Anything to keep your arrest rate up, I suppose. So glad that I can be of use.'

'We're not going to pin anything on you, Shane. You are very neatly wrapped up.'

'For what?'

'Murder. Get dressed, please, you're coming down town with us.'

'Rather wished that you'd told us, Jim,' said the voice on the other end of the line. 'We've been watching that house for some time.'

'Constantly?'

'No. On and off—otherwise we would have seen you go in. Let's say we've been keeping a wee eye on the building and its occupants.'

'I really don't think that we did any damage,' said King.

46

'They thought that we were Drug Squad, but we disabused them of that notion.'

'You didn't search, then?'

'No.' King leaned forward and rested his elbows on his desk as he tended to do when undertaking a difficult telephone conversation. His courtesy call to the Drug Squad to inform them of the panic that he had caused at the given address had not met with the thanks that he had anticipated. 'No,' he repeated, 'we had no grounds for a search warrant.'

'So who did you lift?'

'Shane Dodemaide.'

'Ratty?'

'Is that his nickname?'

'It's our name for him. Don't tell him or you'll hurt his feelings. We've given nicknames to half a dozen or so in that house for rapid ID among ourselves, so that we know who we are talking about.'

'I see. We also pulled an Irish girl, Sadie Kelly.'

'Yes. We know her. She's got previous for possession.'

'We're checking her out. She only looks to be about thirteen.'

'She's actually seventeen,' said the sergeant of the Drug Squad. 'She won't carry her birth certificate because she gets pulled on suspicion of being a runaway and if she gets kept in a police station for long enough, she gets fed a free meal. She keeps herself going that way. I also think she enjoys the game. Anyway, you just went in and out.'

'Yes.'

'Saw no one except the two that you huckled?'

'No one.'

'Didn't go into any of the rooms?'

'Only Shane Dodemaide's dive and even then just briefly. Nothing in it; mattress on bare floorboards, a few sheets, a blanket, smell of damp.'

'Was he alone in the room?'

'Yes. Should he not have been?'

'Thought he might have been with his moll—tall, dark-haired girl.'

'No. No, he was alone.'

47

'Fair enough. Can I ask why you lifted him?'

'Wanted in connection with the murder of Eddie Wroe.'

'Eddie . . .' The sergeant of the Drug Squad gasped down the telephone. 'See, those neds—they're like a tank full of Siamese fighting fish. If they're not mugging pensioners, they're mugging each other. Do you know what happened?'

'No. We found Eddie Wroe's body early this morning—' King glanced at his watch: 0023—'that is to say, early yesterday, Sunday, morning, in an alley in the town. Multiple stab wounds, knife beside the body. Knife fitted the wounds. Eddie Wroe's blood on the knife—well, the same blood group anyway, and lo and behold, whose dabs do we find on the weapon?'

'Shane Dodemaide's?'

'The one and the same. Both known to each other, both live in the same squat, both have p.c.'s and Dodemaide in particular has p.c.'s for violence.'

'Pretty well open and shut.'

'Looks that way.'

'Still, it's not Dodemaide's style, if I know Dodemaide. He'll give someone a kicking but I've never known him use a weapon.'

'He's only twenty-one. He's just starting out and it was a particularly frenzied attack, by all accounts. Wroe probably called him "Ratty".'

'So what is Dodemaide saying about it?'

'Not a lot.' King relaxed a little, the angry edge had left the voice of the sergeant of the Drug Squad as it had become clear that little or no damage had been done by the CID. 'He seems shaken, upset, reckons that he and the deceased were mates, reckons he was in bed from eleven p.m. Saturday night until midday Sunday.'

'Alone?'

'Yes. He can't offer an alibi or a witness, and as his only mates all appear to live in that house, then any witness that he might be able to come up with would be of limited credibility. Says he stays in bed late because he gets hungry if he gets up and he can't afford to eat as much as he would like to.'

'I can believe that. All his cash goes on yellow powder that he punctures into his veins. He'll start going into cold turkey in a few hours' time. Won't get any sense out of him then.'

'I'll go and have another chat with him. Can I ask the nature of the Drug Squad's interest in the house?'

'Nothing that we can put our finger on; we jut know the building as a nest of thieves and vipers, all of whom have an unhealthy interest in narcotics. Most are low-lifers, no serious pushers with villas in Spain that we can identify. Most are petty neds and no-hopers from the beginning; one or two are university drop-outs like "the Princess".'

'Who is she?'

'Tall raven-haired beauty of about nineteen summers. She who I would have been expecting, or half-expecting, to share a bed with Dodemaide. She appeared on the scene a few weeks ago, just inside the New Year, and hasn't been seen for a week almost. Nothing to be alarmed about. She became Dodemaide's moll, but has probably dropped back into the University, if she has any sense. We called her the Princess for ready identification. Never got to know her name. All that live in house claim state benefit and spend the night hustling, mugging people, the boys screw cars or turn people's windows, the girls work the street.'

'Some life,' said King.

Elka Willems glanced sideways at the luminous dial of the alarm clock on her bedside cabinet: 01.40. She said, 'Monday, bloody Monday.' She had to report for duty in less than five hours. Sleep evaded her and the more she tried to get to sleep, the more awake she seemed.

Beside her under the duvet Ray Sussock grunted something unintelligible. He was sleepy, on the verge of sleep itself. The wine had made him sleepy, Sunday dinner, a traditional roast, eaten in the evening, assisted by wine. He had handed over to King, leaving the station only when the deceased had been positively identified, and had driven home. Some home, a temporary bedsit in a large house in the West End of Glasgow. He had washed, grabbed a change of clothes, and had then driven over to Langside. He parked his car right at the entrance to the close and went up the stair. The door with the 'Willems' nameplate in gold on a fancy tartan background was two up right. He pressed the bell. She opened the door and smiled at him. Gone was the severe serge uniform and blonde hair tight in a bun. Now she was in tight, figure-hugging jeans and a sweater and her hair fell about her shoulders, a twenty-seven-year-old blonde-haired, blue-eyed Nordic goddess. Dutch on her father's side. She reached forward and hooked a slender finger under the knot of Sussock's tie, tugged him over the threshold and hipped the door shut behind him.

'In you come, old Sussock,' she said.

Later, mid-evening, after the meal, they lay side by side and listened to a woman in high heels click-click beneath their window while upstairs the heavily built middle-aged woman stamped crossly across her floor, their ceiling.

'Heaven only knows what the neighbours think,' she had said, running her slender fingers down his spine, 'we did make a bit of a noise.'

'That's me,' he had murmured into the pillow, 'sixty years old and still a sexual athlete.'

'It's a bit hypocritical,' she giggled, lying back and looking at the ceiling. 'I mean, we're cops—how can we expect people to come quietly if we can't do it ourselves?'

Then she had slumbered. Later, she had awakened. Beside her old Sussock, who had earlier crossed her room looking, she thought, like a potato on stilts, was almost asleep. She was awake.

She tried to grab two hours before the alarm jangled her into resentful activity. She couldn't and lay there feeling cheated of something.

He actually did it. King felt his lips begin to twitch into an unkind grin, almost laughing at a joke in poor taste, but he actually did it. Ratty put the backs of both hands up to his nose and sniffed and blew, as if preening whiskers. King had sat opposite Dodemaide, then stood and addressed him from the corner of the interview room and watched as he sniffed and blew with both hands reversed against his nose.

'Listen, Shane.' King sat again and looked into Dodemaide's frightened eyes. 'You are a young guy, but you've got a lot of previous. That means that you know the score, so you know fine well that when your hide is nailed to the wall, as your hide is right now, then you begin to run out of options. Basically, you've got two . . .'

'I work for myself or I work against myself.' Dodemaide had a low-pitched, hard-edged voice, the voice of someone who felt that life had done him a great injustice. King thought it strange that a deep voice should belong to one so tiny. 'I know these words by heart. I say them in my sleep. Like you said, I've been this way before.'

'So?' King smiled.

'So?'

'So you killed him, and that's it.'

Dodemaide shook his head in a manner which King thought to be smug and detached. 'So I didn't kill him and *that's* it.'

'We found the murder weapon, we found your dabs on the murder weapon, we know that you and Eddie Wroe knew each other.'

'We were mates.'

'You lived in the same gaff, you shot up together, you probably shared each other's works, you turned people's windows together, you screwed people's cars together, you knock little old ladies down to the ground and steal their pensions, and one day you and Eddie had an argument and you stabbed him. You stabbed him and dumped his body in an alley.'

'Did I?' Dodemaide smiled. 'Then you shouldn't have difficulty proving it. I've been here two hours now. You either charge me or let me go.'

'He came at you and you took the knife from him.'

'No, I didn't.'

'Come on, Shane, tell us what happened, help yourself and the charges could be reduced. How does culpable homicide sound—or even manslaughter?'

51

'Sounds good, sounds better than murder. Called plea bargaining, isn't it?'

'So, what happened between you and Eddie Wroe?'

'Nothing. I went to my bed, my mattress, late Saturday, slept late, went up the 'tannies—the Botanical Gardens—in the afternoon and sat in the wind and blew some grass. Came back, shot up, went out . . . came back. Went to bed. Got woken up by you guys. Haven't seen Eddie since Saturday morning. I suppose I won't see him again. He was the sort of guy who'd drift, he'd come, he'd go. You know how it is?'

King shot to his feet and opened the door. A constable entered the room. King said, 'Take him to the charge bar.'

In a large room adjacent to the uniform bar stood a metal desk. A wooden desk with an inclined plane stood on the metal desk. King stood in front of the desk with the plane inclined towards him. Shane Dodemaide stood in front of the desk, hand-cuffed to the constable. King laid papers on the inclined plane of the desk and consulted them. He looked at Dodemaide. 'Are you listening?'

Dodemaide nodded.

'Right, then . . . Prisoner at the bar, you are not obliged to say anything, but anything you do say will be taken down and may be used in evidence . . . do you understand?'

'Aye.' Dodemaide nodded.

'Shane Dodemaide, you are charged that on the night of twenty-eighth March in the city of Glasgow, in the vicinity of Sauchiehall Lane, or elsewhere, you did assault Edward Wroe with a knife, that you did stab him repeatedly all to his hurt and severe injury and did murder him.'

Silence.

King spoke and wrote, 'Prisoner at the bar made no reply.'

CHAPTER 4

Monday, 08.30–18.30 hours

Fabian Donoghue pulled his Rover into the rear of P Division Police Station at Charing Cross and parked in the space marked 'Detective-Inspector'. He glanced at his gold hunter—just forty-five minutes from his home in Edinburgh to his place of work. Not a bad trip at all, fast and smooth, no hold-ups, no delays, just a steady sixty miles an hour. He slipped the watch back into his waistcoat pocket, left his car and walked the short distance across the car park to the door at the rear of the police station itself. He signed in, checked his pigeonhole for messages and went upstairs, taking two at a time, and into the CID corridor. In his office, he took off his coat and homburg and hung them on the coat-stand; he sat down at his desk, ready to begin his day's work at 08.32.

He leaned forward and tore off Saturday and Sunday's date from his desk calendar and read the day's message for Monday, 28th March. It was the Mark Twain quote, 'Giving up something is easy. I've done it many times.' Donoghue smiled and thought it appropriate as he reached for his pipe with the gently curved stem with one hand and his tobacco pouch with the other. He filled his pipe with easy expertise, glancing at the operation only occasionally, but for the most part doing it by practised touch, enjoying as he did so the fragrance from the tobacco as it teased his nostrils. The tobacco he favoured was a special mix, made up especially for him by a small independent tobacconist in the city centre; it had a Dutch base for taste, with a twist of dark shag for depth of flavour and a slower burning rate. He smoked five ounces a week; less than he used to smoke. When the bowl of the pipe had been filled to his satisfaction, he replaced the tobacco pouch in his jacket pocket, took his gold-plated lighter from his waistcoat pocket and played the flame over the bowl of the pipe, drawing the smoke up the stem and blowing it from his mouth with loving satisfaction. It was the first pipe of the day—always the most enjoyable.

He leaned backwards in his chair and glanced out of his office window at the city, looking up the length of Sauchiehall Street, at the shops, the office buildings, at the buses nose to tail, of many different liveries following de-regulation of the services, thus allowing the independent operators to compete with the municipal service. Above the boldly angular buildings of down-town Glasgow, the sky was blue with a few heavy white clouds. Not a bad day at all, for the time of year, and after such a wet weekend. He thought that this year might very well be a good summer and his thoughts drifted momentarily to a week's fishing in the Borders.

A tap on his office door brought him sharply back to reality.

'Come in,' he said.

Montgomerie entered his office and strode confidently towards Donoghue's desk, a number of files under his arm.

'Take a pew, Montgomerie.' Donoghue took the pipe from his mouth and nodded to the chair in front of his desk. He rested his elbows on his desk at either side of the blotting-paper bad. Odd item of office furniture, he thought, utterly and completely redundant since the advent of the ballpoint pen, but without which no desk looks complete. He glanced at Montgomerie and thought that the young detective-constable looked pleased with himself. He also looked tired and bleary-eyed, as would any cop who had just come to the end of the graveyard shift. He looked a little grimy, his downturned moustache—which normally set off his chiselled, aquiline features very well—was now beginning to share his face with a growth which was somewhere between a five o'clock shadow and designer stubble, more of a shadow, not yet quite a stubble, but none the less Montgomerie, Donoghue saw, was evidently the sort of man who has to shave twice a day. Montgomerie smiled through the fatigue, smiled through the stubble. He did indeed look pleased with himself.

'Good weekend, sir?' he asked, sitting as invited. He was a Glasgow man whose gentrified accent betrayed his Bearsden childhood and had been further softened by three terms in the Department of Law at Edinburgh University.

'Pleasant enough, thank you.' Donoghue had an equally soft accent, although he was from the Saracen, the streets of cobbles and high kerbstones, canyons of tenements, pitched battles in the street on a Saturday night. He had fought up the way and had eventually graduated with honours from Glasgow University and, at forty-one years, also spoke with a soft Glasgow accent. 'Didn't get as much done as I would have liked, but as often as not that seems to be the way of it.' He drew gently on his pipe. The preliminaries over, he looked squarely at Montgomerie and then raised an eyebrow.

'Well, sir.' Montgomerie shuffled in the chair and laid the files on his lap. He was well used to Donoghue's method of calling the meeting to order and requesting information. 'Routine weekend, sir.' Montgomerie opened the first file. 'Item one is car thefts. We had a team that stole a car from the car park of Yorkhill Hospital and used it to visit every hospital car park in the West End, and park and ride car parks—well, you name it, we followed their spoor all across the West End as reports came in of car radios and stereos stolen and eventually we found the stolen car abandoned in a side street in the Broomielaw. They got away with hundreds if not thousands of pounds' worth of goodies.'

'How far are we on with that?'

'Not very far, sir. The stolen vehicle is with Forensic right now and they are going over it with a fine-tooth comb, as they say; the first impression is that the thieves wore gloves.'

'Donoghue took his pipe from his mouth. 'So that will have to be allocated.'

'It would seem so, sir.' Montgomerie laid the file on the edge of Donoghue's desk.

'We had the usual gamut of Code 7s, a few people got their windows turned, clean, neat jobs, straight in and out, lifted a few items but didn't vandalize the houses.'

'Some compensation for the home-owner!'

'And by means of compensation for us,' said Montgomerie, 'we pulled a team on suspicion, four boys sitting in a car in a residential area. Took them home and their houses were full of stolen property. We wrapped up twenty reported break-ins with those arrests.'

'Good, very good.'

'They've been released on bail.'

'Very well.' Donoghue wondered when Montgomerie was going to come to the case which was making him look so pleased.

'We also had the usual fights when the dancing chucked them out; the cells are full of neds with some heads and no recollection of how they got to be banged up for the weekend.'

'They rarely have.' Donoghue held the bowl of his pipe in the cupped palms of his hands. 'I think that ninety per cent of crime must be alcohol-related.'

'I'd be inclined to agree, sir,' said Montgomerie, working through the files. 'We had a stabbing in the city centre, not fatal, the assailant fled. And—' he came to the last file— 'we had one Code 41.'

'Only one murder.' Donoghue smiled. 'It *has* been a quiet weekend.'

'Quiet by comparison, sir. This one is wrapped up already, signed, sealed and delivered. Victim identified and a man has been charged.'

'Really!' Donoghue nodded, impressed. 'All on your own, Montgomerie?'

'No, I had no part in it, sir.' Montgomerie handed the case file to Donoghue. 'It's all down to Sergeant Sussock and Richard King.'

'Who made the arrest?'

'Richard King.'

'And he's been charged?'

'Yes, sir.'

'So he'll be going up before the Sheriff this morning and he'll be remanded, pending trial.'

'That's the pattern, sir.'

'Well, it's policy in Scotland not to grant bail to persons charged with murder, as you well know. I wondered why you were looking pleased, Montgomerie.'

'Didn't know it showed, sir, but I am pleased for Sergeant Sussock and Richard.'

'Generous and unselfish of you.'

'Well, I like the Division to keep its end up.'

'As do we all. Look, I know that you want to get away, but could you give me a summary of the circumstances before I look over the file for myself?'

'Well . . .' Montgomerie became uncomfortable.

'I've told you before, Montgomerie—I've told you that if you wanted to punch a time card, then you shouldn't have entered a profession.'

'Yes, sir.'

'So summarize it for me, please!'

'Well, sir, body found by a beat cop, yesterday morning in the city centre—'

'The city centre?'

'An alley behind Sauchiehall Street, Sauchiehall Lane at West Nile Street.'

'I see.'

'Subsequently identified as one Eddie Wroe, a druggie, lives in a squat with a few similar personages.'

'Where at?'

'Belmont Street, Kelvinbridge. Knife found near the body. Wroe died of stab wounds—the knife has been identified as the likely murder weapon.'

'You mean it fits the wounds?'

'Yes, sir, Dr Reynolds was able to test the knife late yesterday, and the blood group of the blood on the knife is the same as the victim's blood group. The knife had fingerprints on the handle which were identified as belonging to one Shane Dodemaide—'

'So we know him.'

'Yes, theft, violence—and he lived at the same address

57

as Eddie Wroe. Richard King picked him up last night. He denied everything, as one would expect, but he was charged anyway.'

'I see.' Donoghue pulled on his pipe. 'Clear-cut, as you say.'

'It seems to me to be so, sir. Open and shut, really. Will that be all, sir?'

'Were you able to identify a motive at all?'

'I don't believe so, sir. The other thing you should know is that the Drug Squad is interested in the building, or rather the occupants of same; we didn't know that last night, so Richard King told me at the shift change-over. It rattled their cage a bit that we went in without notifying them, but we had no reason to suspect that we'd be treading on any toes. In the event, we did no damage and the Drug Squad is still talking to us. They are just keeping an eye on the premises.'

'Thank you. I'll bear that in mind.'

'Will that be all, sir?'

'Yes. Thank you, Montgomerie.'

The woman knelt beside the girl who sat on the bed, her knees pulled up to her chest. Her eyes were wide, her mouth set firm in a teeth-clenching grimace, her hands clutching her stomach. The woman reached out and rested a hand comfortingly on the girl's feet. She said, 'It won't be long now. Father knows best. He knows what he's doing.'

Donoghue read the report of the arrest and charging of Shane Dodemaide. He then appraised himself of all other incidents reported to the P Division CID over the weekend and reports of all other CID investigations and arrests. Then, for a second time, he read the file on the murder of Eddie Wroe and the subsequent arrest of Shane Dodemaide.

He didn't like it. He didn't like it when he first read it and when he read it for the second time, he liked it even less. Donoghue slowly and carefully refilled his pipe and played the flame of the lighter over the bowl, adding more smoke to the layers of smoke which were already beginning to fill his office. He rose from his desk and switched on the electric fan which stood on top of the grey Scottish Office issue filing cabinet. He resumed his seat. He couldn't put his finger on why he didn't like the report, and he had to concede that it was all there—a relationship of sorts between victim and accused which he felt was very, very relevant because in over twenty years of police service Donoghue had only once dealt with a random stabbing.

A boy, a teenager, was waiting at a bus stop and another boy of about the same age was walking along the road with his mates; as he drew level with the bus stop, he drew a knife and stabbed the boy who was waiting for a bus. Just like that. Didn't know the young man from Adam; no preamble, no cross words, not even any eye contact; nothing. Stab. You're dead. He didn't intend to kill him, so he said, just rip him a bit. Just. None the less, he went down for life and, to Donoghue's mind, deservedly so. He remembered the young man, the murderer, being exceptionally self-important, not a thought about the boy he had wantonly murdered, not a thought for the family he had devastated, not even a thought for the effect on his own family. He just wanted to know how long he would have to wait before he got a cell of his own.

On this occasion Eddie Wroe had been stabbed repeatedly, so it probably wasn't random, and he and Shane Dodemaide knew each other and the motivation for the crime ought to be able to be located within their relationship. Dodemaide had stabbed Eddie Wroe in a garage or similar premises, had dumped the corpse in the city and had gone home, only to be wakened by the law a few hours later and huckled for murder. And why not? The murder weapon was found almost next to the body with Shane Dodemaide's fingerprints on it.

Too neat. Too neat by half.

Donoghue reclined in his chair. No, he thought, no, it isn't too neat at all; it's clumsy; glaringly, obviously flawed. A man who kills another in one place and removes the body to a place where it is intended to be found would dispose of the murder weapon. If then, Donoghue reasoned, the

59

weapon was found close to the body, it was only found because it was meant to be found. And, as a consequence, Shane Dodemaide's fingerprints were also meant to be found.

So Dodemaide had been set up. By whom?

'Answer that one, Fabian,' said Donoghue, as he stood and reached for his hat and coat. 'Answer that and you've got your man.'

He walked into the town for lunch.

Montgomerie drained his glass. He was sitting alone in the re-vamped Rock on Highburgh Road. A group of business men sat in the corner, another man sat alone in the middle of the room, reading an early edition of the *Evening Times*. In another corner two women sat in front of tall glasses and talked to each other, and both, it seemed to Montgomerie, seemed to be talking at the same time. The lunch-time rush had died down, just the stragglers remained. Outside it was overcast and grey, already heralding the evening.

He had left P Division police station, finally clearing the building at 09.30 hours after being obliged to indulge what he had always felt to be the Detective-Inspector's favourite game of 'kicking it around a bit'. He'd driven home to his flat just off Highburgh Road, three up and overlooking the swing park, washed, changed and had walked down to Byres Road to the supermarket at the top of the road and bought a plastic bag full of food. On the way back to his flat he'd called in at the Rock, just one to help him sleep, he had told himself. A glass of Guinness.

It went down very well. Very well indeed. In fact, it didn't touch the sides of his throat.

So he had another.

He got into conversation with a merchant seaman and they began to buy each other drinks. The waitress came up with a smile and a cloth and cleared their table of empty glasses and wiped the ashtray clean. Then the merchant seaman said he had to go, by which time Montgomerie could not remember how much he had had to drink. The clean table and the clean ashtray deluded him into thinking that it probably hadn't been that much. Not really much at all.

So he bought another pint of Guinness and it slipped down like silk.

It's always the way of it, he thought, always; he could go for days without a drink and not crave one, but if he took one and he got the taste, then he went on until he was legless. He sat and cradled the glass in his lap and he wondered if he maybe had a wee problem.

Sussock sat in the chair in front of Donoghue's desk. Donoghue smiled warmly at Sussock but thought privately that the Detective-Sergeant looked too old for the job, certainly too old for the street. He was coming up sixty, he'd won extended service, he had a thin, craggy face and a permanently tired look in his eyes.

'I had a glance at the file on the Eddie Wroe murder before I went to lunch.' Donoghue lit his pipe. 'I can't pretend that I'm happy, Ray; the first impressions weren't good. I mulled it over in my mind over lunch—over my plaice and chips—and I came back and read it again, very carefully and I'm now even less happy.'

'Oh?' Sussock was genuinely disappointed. 'I thought it was very neat.' He coughed as the smoke from Donoghue's pipe reached his chest.

'That's just it, Ray. You've hit the nail on the head. It's too neat, it clicks along like a game of snooker until the black ball rolls smoothly into the pocket.'

'But it's all there, sir.' Sussock grasped at straws. He needed an achievement, if only for his own self-respect, let alone his professional credibility. 'Murder weapon with Dodemaide's dabs all over it, a relationship within which will be the motive . . . It seems to me, sir, that all the questions have been answered, all i's dotted and t's crossed.'

'Well, not quite, Ray, not quite. Let me share my doubts with you.' Donoghue drew deeply on his briar and blew the smoke out of his mouth and noted the look of resignation which fell across the face of the older man. 'I'm sorry to shove a spoke in your wheel, Ray, but the sooner we get it right, the less we fall, the less stupid we look. Well, in the first instance, we have an impression that the murder was impulsive, frenzied, that the locus was the location where the body was found, and that the murderer, having stabbed Eddie Wroe a number of times, ran away in a panic and threw the weapon away as he did so. Is that a fair summation, Ray?'

'Yes, sir.'

'Now, for me—' Donoghue sat back in his chair and Sussock, paraphrasing Conan Doyle, began to feel a suspicion that this meeting was going to develop into a three-pipe kick-about—'for me,' repeated Donoghue, 'it doesn't gel. It doesn't gel at all. You see, we have evidence that the murder took place elsewhere and that is the key; at least I would respectfully submit that that is the key. Rigor had set in while the body was prostrate face upwards, that is clear from the pathologist's report. Clear from the Forensic report is that the body had lain where the denim clothing had become impregnated with oil, grease, metal filings, etcetera, etcetera. Dr Kay suggests the floor of a garage. So we have to assume that Eddie Wroe was slain in a garage and that he lay where he was slain for up to twelve hours before being moved to the place where he was subsequently found by PC Hamilton. Is that a fair assumption, do you feel?'

'Yes, sir.' Sussock shuffled in his seat and waited with educated and accustomed patience while his senior lovingly played the flame of his lighter over the bowl of his pipe.

'So—' Donoghue snapped the chunky gold-plated lighter shut and slipped it into his waistcoat pocket—'a dead weight, literally a dead weight, was moved. Now we'll come on to that in a moment, but for the time being, we have a body that was dumped in a place different from the place at which it became life extinct and the apparent murder weapon was found a few feet away from where the body lay.'

Sussock nodded. 'I see what you are driving at, sir.'

'Good. It is a rather obvious flaw, isn't it? You move a

murder victim only to conceal your own foul hand in the deed. You do not also move the murder weapon and leave it placed conveniently next to the body, especially not when it is covered with your fingerprints.'

'The only reason why anybody would want to do that,' said Sussock, embarrassed at his own lack of insight, 'would be to point the finger of suspicion at another person. In this case, Shane Dodemaide.'

'That,' said Donoghue, nodding with approval, 'is my view entirely.' He drew on his pipe. The sweet-smelling tobacco filled the room and continued a relentless attack on Sussock's crusted lungs. It was the end of March, soon it would be May, the merry month, soon he would have three or even four months of a pain-free chest until the thin winter air began to swirl about Glasgow again, usually around October. 'I am glad we are agreed, but just to emphasize the point, I have here the post-mortem report on Eddie Wroe. He stood five ten and weighed eleven stone. Not a small man. In fact, he was quite large by West of Scotland standards. Now you have had the opportunity to interview Shane Dodemaide?'

'Ratty, as the Drug Squad call him. Yes, sir. Well, no, I haven't interviewed him, but I saw him when he was taken from the cells to the Sheriff Court this morning.'

'What's he like?'

'Small, spindly, puny in a word.'

'Is he capable of carrying a corpse like the corpse of Eddie Wroe would have been—large and heavy?'

'No, sir,' Sussock conceded. 'Not without an accomplice or a motor vehicle.'

'Do you know if he can drive?'

'I don't, sir.'

'Or if he has access to a vehicle?'

'Again, sir, I don't know.'

'So can you imagine the sort of mince and tatties that even a half-baked defence would make of the prosecution case of Shane Dodemaide as it stands at present?'

'As it stands at present, sir, the Fiscal will lob it out of the window—it won't even get to court.'

'I'm glad we are agreed.' Donoghue settled back in his chair. He pulled on his pipe and then took it from his mouth and examined the bowl with a look of annoyance. Then, to Sussock's immense relief and surprise, laid the thing in the huge glass ashtray that stood on the right-hand side of his desk. 'So where do we go from here? I have the feeling not of being robbed of something but of having just escaped the deepest of public humiliations. We have succeeded in weeding the garden. What are we left with?'

'A body, sir.'

'Anything else?'

'Well, evidence that he was probably killed in a garage and moved—'

'Yes, yes,' Donoghue said testily. 'Think people, Ray, people. The weeds have hidden a few fruit-bearing plants. What I mean is, if Shane Dodemaide was deliberately placed under suspicion by the murderer, then it is not unreasonable to assume that the murderer must have been known to both Eddie Wroe and Shane Dodemaide in some capacity.'

'Ah.' Sussock nodded.

'So there is a link between them and it ain't that one murdered t'other, 'tis something a wee bitty more tenuous, but it's a link. Eddie Wroe was not a small man—he wasn't a powerfully built man either—so it's reasonable to assume that his assailant had some beef about him.'

'And access to a garage.'

'Yes, and the means to take or to lure Eddie Wroe to his place of most unlawful execution.'

'A large man or men, with a vehicle?'

'Motive?'

'As yet unknown, sir. But once we have established the link between Eddie Wroe and Shane Dodemaide—'

'A link more than the fact that they shared the same damp squat and hypodermic syringes.'

'Yes, sir, but as soon as we establish that link, I think we'll also find a motive.'

'So what's to be done, Ray?'

'Well, sir, I think that we should pursue the only lead

that we have, we should have a chat with Shane Dodemaide and visit their place of abode.'

Donoghue glanced at the clock on his office wall. 'Sixteen-thirty hours. We'll do that tomorrow, I think, Ray.' He picked up his pipe, tapped the burnt ash into the ashtray and began to refill. 'I don't think that it will do Mr Dodemaide any harm to spend a few days in youth custody. It'll focus his mind on the issue of the direction that his life is taking. It'll bring him down to earth. I know he's been in the can before, but it's never comfortable. We'll visit him tomorrow morning. He should be well strung out by then. Who's drawn what shifts this week?'

'I'm on day shift, as you see. King is on the back shift, starting in thirty minutes in fact, and Montgomerie's drawn the graveyard shift.'

'Good. Have King see me as soon as he comes in. Thank you, Ray. I'll see you tomorrow.' Donoghue lit his pipe.

Sussock left the office, sparing his tortured lungs any more unnecessary suffering.

'Aye, son, you know he's done a few daft things in his life but he'd never kill anyone.' The woman sat in the chair in a near-catatonic state. Only her mouth seemed to move, her eyes stared straight ahead and her body and her hands and her feet never moved even a fraction of an inch, not at least that Richard King was able to detect. He had arrived for the back shift at 17.00, sat at his desk, his phone had rung, Sergeant Sussock informing him that DI Donoghue wished to speak with him.

'It's the murder case, Richard,' Donoghue had said as he fastened his light-coloured raincoat and reached for his homburg. 'It's not as clear-cut as Ray Sussock and you first thought, so I think we need a little background information on who appeared to be our prime suspect, Shane Dodemaide—visit his home, Richard, visit his squat.'

'I'll have to clear that with the Drug Squad, sir. The visit to the squat, I mean.'

'All taken care of, Richard.' Donoghue screwed his hat

on to his head. 'I pointed out to them that a murder inquiry rather takes priority over most everything else.'

'They couldn't argue with that, sir.'

'They couldn't and they didn't.' Donoghue had smiled. 'It was all very amicable, though. If you could record anything of interest or relevance—a hand-written report will suffice for the time being. If you could crack on to that on this shift.'

King had driven out to the Saracen, to the address that Shane Dodemaide had given as his home address when charged. He left the car on the main drag and walked up Killearn Street, a wide street of low-rise inter-war housing, dark and forbidding. A group of neds stood and watched him from the shadows—only one in three street lamps were working. He missed his car, but felt that it was better left on the main street. Once the word got round that there was an unattended police motor sitting in the shadows, then there wouldn't be a great deal left for him to return to. Nothing that was driveable anyway. He climbed the concrete steps up to the door of the fifth close. The newly installed controlled entry system had already been vandalized and broken. He opened the door, the stair was dull, maroon paint up to shoulder height, cream thereafter, heavily covered with graffiti, mostly on the cream. The door with 'Dodemaide' embossed in gold on tartan nameplate was first floor left. King had pressed the buzzer. It didn't work. He rapped on the door. It was opened almost immediately by a young woman.

'Aye,' she had said.

'Police,' King had said and watched the young woman's eyes harden.

'I'd like to talk to Shane Dodemaide's parents or family.'

'Well, I'm his wee sister, his ma's in the room.' The young woman was thinly built, about seventeen years old, King thought. She had dark, closely cropped hair, wore denims and pink stiletto shoes. She had cheap tattoos on her forearm. The hallway behind her was dark and smelled heavily of damp. 'You'd better come in.'

She led King down the corridor to the living-room of the

house. The living-room had a wall to wall carpet that was sticky to walk on; a naked light bulb hung from the ceiling; in the grate old bits of furniture burned, flame licked at the varnish of an old chair leg. It was a flame, but it gave little heat. In the corner of the room was a bed and lying on the bed, under dirty blankets, was an old woman with long straggly silver hair and a craggy, bearded face. In an upright dining chair by the fire was a woman, younger than the woman in the bed but older than the woman who had answered the door; she had the same worn and wasted features as the older woman. The woman in the chair didn't glance up as King entered the room. King looked at the curtainless windows. It was now dark, night had fallen and rain was beginning to fall.

'The polis, Ma,' said the girl. She turned to King. 'That's my ma in the chair. On the bed, that's my gran. She's got cancer, so she has.'

'I'm sorry,' said King, surprised at the girl's lack of sensitivity.

'She can't hear,' the girl said, by means of explanation. She left the room, closing the door behind her.

King had addressed the woman in the chair, who seemed to be mesmerized by the blue-yellow flame licking hungrily at the varnish of the old chair leg, a small flame which seemed to King to be clinging to life just like the old deaf woman in the bed in the corner.

'It's about Shane.' His breath hung in the air as he spoke.

'Aye,' the woman said slowly. 'When I had the polis at my door in the middle of the night wanting to know if he stayed here, I knew there was more trouble. I told them he didn't stay here, but it was his home, if you ken. He normally stays in a flat in the West End.'

'It's a squat,' said King, shivering as the insiduous cold of the room began to reach his bones. 'We can't accept it as an address. That's why you got knocked up in the night. You know that he's been charged with murder?'

'Aye.' The woman continued to stare into the fire. 'Aye, son, he's done a few daft things in his time but he'd never kill anyone. See, my eldest boy died in a stabbing; my man—he died in an accident in the house and that was by a knife as well—bled all over this carpet and I haven't been able to get all the blood up yet; that was ten years ago. Now Shane, he's in gaol for stabbing someone. See, knives, son, they kill me, so they do.'

'When did Shane move out?'

'When he turned sixteen, just as soon as he could. He didn't get on with me and I didn't get one with him. He was bad, he was my son, but he was bad. But he's not so bad that he'd kill anybody, so he isn't.'

'Bad?' King remained standing. The tacky carpet was sufficient warning against sitting on the settee.

'Bad, aye, bad. He got into the glue, got into the lighter fluid, got into the hairspray; went into a List D for house-breaking and he was still only thirteen. Never got out. He just used his leave to sniff glue, turn people's windows, screw cars and steal from shops.' Mrs Dodemaide continued to stare into the fire, only her mouth moved and even then she spoke in a monotone. On the bed, the old woman who had so far remained silent began to wheeze and cough and splutter. Then she fell silent again. 'So he came home at sixteen, stayed for a day and then went into a flat in the West End. Not the same one he's in now, but that was him, just moved from flat to flat, never knew what he did with his time. That was about four years ago. Have you been where he stays now?'

'Aye,' King said. 'Did Shane ever mention a guy called Eddie Wroe?'

Mrs Dodemaide shook her head. 'No, sir,' she said. 'Who's that?'

'Just another guy who lives at the same squat as Shane, at least he did until he was stabbed to death.'

'So he's the guy that Shane was supposed to have killed.' The woman shook her head. 'No, he never mentioned that name to me. He left at sixteen, but he never really stayed here since he was thirteen. Not like his other brother. His other brother stuck by his ma until he was stabbed in the town one night. Aye, Tommy—he was a good boy, so he was. Worked at the Casino as a doorman in a smart red uniform. Done really well for himself, so he did. See, the trouble with Shane is that he never had a father.'

'Oh?'

'Not to speak of.' The woman continued to stare at the thin flame as it curled around the chair leg. 'See, to let you understand, his dad was a rat. That's when all my troubles started, twenty years ago when I married a rat. You know what happened to him right here in this room?'

'He died in an accident,' said King. 'You said so.'

'He walked out on me when Shane was five and Tracy couldn't even walk, but he kept popping back. It was when he called back, full of the drink, Shane was about ten, he came into the room carrying a knife, tripped on the carpet and fell on it—went right through his heart, so it did—blood everywhere. After that I was on my own. I was shot of the rat, but I never met another man so I brought the kids up alone, by myself on the social security. We never had a lot of spare pennies, so we didn't.' The woman fell silent as if recalling old memories. Then she continued in the same dull monotone. 'Mind, son, I learned from it and I told my kids how to carry a knife if they were walking with it—hold it by the handle with the blade pointing upwards and beside or behind you. I dinned it into them till they did it automatically, polite as well as safe. It meant that if they ever handed a knife to someone, they hadn't to turn it the proper way, handle first.'

'You don't say,' said King. 'You don't say.'

CHAPTER 5

Monday, 18.00–23.30 hours

Sussock sat in the armchair and considered the room; his home. It was small, with a single window which looked out on to an elevated lawn. In one corner was his bed, a divan with a fitted sheet and duvet. He had a second sheet and duvet cover and interchanged them weekly, or as near weekly as he could manage. There was a small table and a chest of drawers on the other wall and a chair in front of the table. He sat in the one armchair in the room. He found it preferable to lying on the bed staring at the ceiling.

There were times that the bedsit seemed like a cell, where he would wake up and feel the walls closing, crushing in on him with all his life's failures. It was a cell that he could leave in order to use the toilet which he shared with others on the landing and he could leave it to use the kitchen.

It was a cell which he shared; in a sense. Once-large rooms had been divided by paper-thin panelling into two or more bedsitting-rooms which sound polluted badly. Consequently, Sussock was obliged to share his room with the two office juniors who had the room above his and whose hi-fi boom-boom-boomed down through his ceiling. The two boys lived together, they had thin faces with piercing eyes and earrings dangling and wore jerseys tucked into their tight jeans, and their grunts and gasps when they coupled were more distasteful to Sussock's ears than the screams and sighs of sexual activity of the more mainstream kind which polluted from the opposite wall. The couple who lived through the opposite wall always seemed to be screaming; it seemed to Sussock as he lay alone in bed or sat in his chair, that either they screamed in sexual ecstasy or screamed in uncontrolled anger. It was one of those relationships.

He survived in the old house largely because of the shift system which meant that he was able to sleep during the day when the house was at its quietest, but mainly he survived because he had to. At an age when most men are moving gracefully and with dignity and gratitude towards retirement, comfortably financially consolidated, he was fighting noise in a cramped room within a house which was populated by children. It was no place for a man of his years.

He grew hungry. He rose from the chair and descended the vast staircase to the kitchen. Fortunately it was empty.

Empty of people, empty of youths crushing and pushing and jostling. Beyond the kitchen, down steep steps and around a dark corner was the landlord's lair. For the first few weeks of Sussock's residence in the huge building, the landlord, a hump-backed, shuffling, sniffling Pole with a Belsen gaze in his eyes, had always seemed to creep up from nowhere, emerging out of the shadows and disappearing back into the gloom and recesses and would especially appear each Saturday morning, hand outstretched. Sussock had always assumed that the man let himself silently into the building, sliding a well-oiled key into a heavily oiled lock. Then, one day, Sussock had occasion to ask the shuffling Pole for a light-bulb and was coldly summoned to the kitchen and then summoned to follow the man down the steps and around the corner, and he thought he was being led to a storeroom. He had always assumed that the landlord lived in sumptuous elegance in Bearsden, among the ancient tribe of Volvo and Mercedes, but in the deep basement of the house he was astounded to find no store room but rather where the landlord and his fat wife lived, not unlike Jack Spratt and spouse. In the landlord's room was a table and four upright chairs; a television stood on the draining-board of the sink unit. At the table sat the landlord's wife and she blinked disapprovingly at Sussock from the gloom of this room in which they existed during the daytime. At night they evidently retired to the room beyond, in which Sussock could see a double bed and nothing else, there being little room for anything else. The landlord had handed Sussock a 60 watt light-bulb and nodded for him to go. So he went, round the dark corner and up the steep steps into the kitchen. He didn't like them, they lived a dim, spartan existence and they had a cold, ungiving attitude, but their living conditions were no better than those of their tenants. No matter what their shortcomings, no one could level a charge of hypocrisy against them.

That incident had taken place much earlier in his residence and now, in the blessedly empty kitchen, Sussock still on a voyage of discovery about the house, found that someone had pilfered his food. He had learned earlier that it was a fatal mistake to keep a large stock of food in a shared kitchen, but to take his last teabag, his last piece of cheese, his last can of beans, all of which had been present when he had last visited the kitchen less than twenty-four hours ago, was too bad.

He went back up to his room. He pulled on his battered raincoat and equally battered old trilby. He glanced into his wardrobe; just subsistence clothing really, mostly winter clothing. Pretty soon he'd need summer clothing. He locked his door and went to Byres Road and bought a quarter-pounder with cheese, coffee and a Danish. Hardly substantial, but it filled a gap. He walked back up to the old house where it nestled behind the trees and got into his old Ford. He drove to the other side of the water, to Rutherglen, just as darkness came and a light drizzle fell diagonally across the yellow sodium street lamps.

Monday night. Glasgow in the rain.

Richard King drove to the squat on Belmont Street. He parked the battered police department heap in a wet gutter and once again smelled the dampness of the houses at the bottom end of the street. To his right as he approached the door of the squat were the bright lights of Great Western Road shimmering in the drizzle, the bars, the fish and chip shop, the kebab takeaway, the trendy shops selling knick-knacks, the charity shops selling second-hand clothing. He noticed a lot of young people about here, denim and long hair, many of whom carried the musty smell of bedsit land about with them. King walked up the short, greasy, slippery path and rapped on the door of the squat. It was opened, but only eventually, and even then with a leisureliness which King thought was just a spit short of contempt.

'You going to feel my collar again?' asked Sadie Kelly, aged seventeen, Irish, who still looked thirteen.

'Not unless you give me a good reason to do so,' said King. 'Are you?'

'Am I what?'

'Going to give me a good reason to feel your collar?'

'Hadn't planned to,' said the short Irish girl. 'What can I do for you?'

'I'd like to come in,' King said. 'I'd like a chat about a few things.'

Sadie Kelly hesitated. King looked behind her into the gloomy hallway. A figure scurried dimly in the dark. She was there to stall the law.

'Do you have a warrant?'

'I can get one.' He pushed past her.

Sadie Kelly let out a howl of protest. King turned.

'Enough of your game-playing. Besides, it's cold and wet outside. In here it's only cold.' The figure continued to scurry upstairs. 'You!' King snapped. 'You! Down here!'

The figure hesitated and then turned and stood on the stairway.

'Lights on!' King addressed Sadie Kelly.

She hesitated.

'Lights!' King allowed an edge to creep into his voice. Sadie Kelly turned, extended an arm and switched on the lightswitch which King saw was loosely attached to the damp plaster. He thought that if the building did not fall down it would likely burn down, and if it didn't burn down the occupants would eventually electrocute themselves. Some building. Even the floorboards felt spongy underfoot. He turned to the figure on the stair, who in the sudden flood of light was revealed as a boy of about nineteen or twenty. He had a thin and wasted appearance and King by now would not have been surprised if the boy was in fact a man of thirty. The boy was not a member of the household that King had previously encountered.

'Who are you?' he asked.

'Nick,' said the youth, blinking.

'Nick who?'

'McQueen. Nick McQueen.'

'Where are you from, Nick McQueen?'

'Clydebank.'

'All right, come down and join us, Nick McQueen from Clydebank.'

McQueen descended the stair and stood in the hallway

underneath the dim naked light-bulb. Close up, he seemed to be about Sadie Kelly's age, about seventeen.

'Who else is in the house?'

'No one,' said Sadie Kelly.

'Just us,' said Nick McQueen.

'Big house for just two people.'

'Well, there was a bit more of us until a couple of days ago,' said Sadie Kelly. 'Besides, we can't live in all of it. The top floor is like a no-go-area—the roof pretty well doesn't exist—and the lower floors are overrun with mice.'

'Yes,' said Nick McQueen. 'It's a bit empty now. There were five of us until a few days ago; now there's two. There was Veronica, there was Eddie and there was Shane. Eddie's dead, you've got Shane in the gaol, and Veronica has just disappeared. She just left. She came like that, just walked in off the street with two plastic bags full of possessions wound round each wrist, saying she heard that there were rooms here. She took the only liveable room left, a small room on the first floor, at the back. Damp, I mean damp, but not as damp as other parts of the house. She slept on a mattress that was rotten underneath.'

'When did she leave?'

'About a week ago. Maybe less. She was kind of posh.'

'She'd been at university,' said Sadie Kelly. 'She was a law student.'

'She'd dropped out,' said Nick McQueen. 'Dropped out of the University, dropped in here and dropped out again. We never knew her second name.'

'Was she a smack-head too?'

Silence.

'Come on, do you think I came up the Clyde on a banana boat? I know what's going on here and I'm not bothered. I'm not Drug Squad. Like I always say, we can talk here or we can talk at the station. So, was she a druggie like Eddie was, and like Shane who is presently strung out in a cell in Longriggend, and like you two are?'

'Yes, she was,' said Sadie Kelly.

Nick McQueen remained silent and looked disappointedly at Sadie Kelly.

'OK,' said King. 'I'm glad we've established that. So what was the connection between Eddie Wroe and Shane Dodemaide?'

'They were mates,' said Nick McQueen. 'They were really good mates. Shane wouldn't have stabbed Eddie.'

'So who did?'

Nick McQueen shrugged his shoulders. 'Don't know, but it wasn't Shane.'

'When did you last see Eddie?'

'Saturday morning. He went out. Said he had to go and see someone and then he was going to look for Veronica.'

'Why would he want to do that?'

'Why wouldn't he?' said McQueen, somewhat to King's annoyance.

'Let's get this clear. Are you telling me that there was something going on between Eddie Wroe and the mysterious Veronica, surname unknown?'

'Yes.' Sadie Kelly shuffled her feet. 'See, Veronica was a classy chick. She came here strung out and Eddie gave her some horse. She just got into the habit of nipping him for it.'

'Nipping him?'

'Sleeping with him. If she slept with him, he gave her all the horse she needed—well, not all. He kept her strung out a wee bit, kept her hungry. She went along with it, otherwise she'd have had to work the street like I have to. She was a classier piece than ever he could pull, I mean wealthy background, nice way of speaking, good looks, tall, everything in proportion, black hair. She was a real dark-haired beauty with track marks running down her arms and legs, and wrists like Crew Junction. She'd tried to top herself at some point.'

'So Eddie was a bit put out that Veronica had walked out on him,' said King. 'So he went looking for her?'

'Most every day. Last time he went out looking for her was Saturday there. Next thing we knew, Shane got huckled last night for his murder. Doesn't add up, sure it doesn't.'

'So, no bad blood between Eddie and Shane?'

'No, not that I was aware of,' said Sadie Kelly.

'Nor me,' said Nick McQueen.

'What about Veronica and Eddie or Veronica and Shane? Anything there?'

'Nothing to speak of. Rows like any couple, but nothing really serious. He never battered her, so he didn't.'

'I'd like to see their rooms.'

King's request was met with a stony and sullen silence. He looked hard at Sadie Kelly and raised his eyebrows. Sadie Kelly turned and went upstairs. King followed her. Nick McQueen followed King. Sadie Kelly opened a door on a gloomy landing.

'This,' she said, 'is where Eddie lived.' She stood aside and allowed King to enter the room. He switched the light on. He thought that the occupant of the room had lived an empty life. He had seen it all before. The inevitable mattress on the floor, the dirty, crumpled sheets and blankets and a blue sleeping-bag and cheap clothing strewn around the floor made the room look like a stall in Paddy's market. He noticed that some of the clothing was female clothing.

'Veronica didn't take all her clothing?' he said. 'So she left in a bit of a hurry after all?'

'I hadn't noticed them,' said Sadie, with a predatory gleam in her eye.

King crossed the room to a chest of drawers and pulled the drawers open one by one, bottom to top. The first three drawers contained radios and hi-fi's torn from the fascias of cars and attested to the method by which the late Eddie Wroe raised money to feed his habit. The top drawer contained the deceased's 'works', hypodermic syringes with broken rusty needles and a series of packages of tightly wrapped tinfoil. He hesitantly and delicately began to sift through the papers at the bottom of the drawer, beyond the hypodermics. One sheet of paper was a pale yellow summons to appear before the Glasgow Sheriff Court to answer a charge of theft by opening lock-fast premises. A second piece of paper clipped to the summons was a letter from a firm of solicitors, Bentley and Co., Bath Street, advising E. Wroe,

Esq. of details of an appointment to discuss the forthcoming appearance before the Glasgow Sheriff. King shut the drawer.

'I've clocked the radios in there,' he said. 'We'll be round later to recover them as stolen property, as yet of unidentified ownership.'

'Yes, sir,' said Sadie disinterestedly, still casting a keenly anticipatory eye over Veronica's clothing.

'We expect them still to be here when we return.'

'They'll be here,' said McQueen with a voice of calm assurance.

'Good. Where did Shane Dodemaide sleep?'

'He'll show you,' said Sadie Kelly, advancing on Veronica's abandoned clothing.

Nick McQueen showed King to a second room further into the gloom of the long landing. King found the room to be a virtual carbon copy of Eddie Wroe's room. Two empty lives living out of each other's rooms. Again female clothing lay among the male clothing.

'Veronica nip Shane Dodemaide as well?' asked King.

'Reckon she must have done,' said Nick McQueen. 'I mean, it was either that or the street. I reckon Sadie will clean up after her. She doesn't have much in the way of clothing and it's cold in here at nights. Sadie doesn't get a lot of new clothing. She doesn't get a lot of new anything.'

King said, 'Show me Veronica's room.'

McQueen said, 'Why?'

'Just do it.'

'Veronica's room was even more naked than the rooms of Eddie Wroe or Shane Dodemaide. Just a mattress on the floor and a torn and crumpled sleeping-bag. A cardboard box contained an old woollen jumper. Presumably, thought King, it was the one item of abandoned clothing that Sadie Kelly did not require. He crossed the soft bare floorboards and opened a cupboard door. Empty. He approached the window but didn't go right up to it, being conscious of the rear wall of the property just two doors away which had collapsed in the night, hingeing from the bottom like a solid

77

sheet of brickwork. He looked out on to the bridge that was Kelvinbridge, the Academy and the lights of Great Western Road. 'So what happened to Veronica?'

McQueen said, 'Like I told you. She just left.'

'Did you see her go?'

'Well, no.'

'Anybody see her go?'

'No.'

'Do you know what her second name is, or was?'

'No. She was just Veronica.'

'Some help you are, Nick McQueen of Clydebank.'

McQueen shrugged his shoulders.

King opened his notebook and took out his ballpoint. 'So her name is or was Veronica. Age?'

'Twenties.'

'Early or late? The twenties are a fast time of life.'

'Early, I suppose.'

'You suppose.' King scribbled in the notebook. 'When did she come to live here?'

'Two months ago. In the middle of winter.'

'And she left last week?'

'Aye, sometime last week.'

'And she was a smack-head?'

'Aye, she shot up two, three times a day. She didn't work the street, sort of too well born for that, but she was sliding that way, they all end up on the street sooner or later if they don't have a supply from another source.'

'But she did?'

'Seemed like it: Eddie or Shane.'

'Or both. But not from you?'

'She didn't want it from me,' he said with a note of disappointment.

'Tell me about her wrists.'

'Like Sadie said, they were criss-crossed like Crew Junction. Fairly old scar tissue though, no sign of stitching. She must have tried to top herself a good few years ago. It wasn't a recent attempt.'

'You some kind of expert?'

McQueen pulled up his right shirtsleeve and showed

78

King his own wrist; it was criss-crossed with a series of linear scars. 'It was a bit like that,' he said.

'Point taken,' said King. 'How old is that?'

'Three years.'

'OK. But she never did anything like that here?'

'No.'

'What else do you know about her?'

'What else do you want to know?'

King paused. He drew breath and exhaled it. 'Where did she come from? She didn't just walk in off the street.'

'I think Shane brought her here, either Shane or Eddie, one or the other. Gave her the spare room, traded smack for her body.'

Above them the roof leaked.

King left the squat, thinking only of the warmth of his own home, of the warmth of Rosemary, his beloved wife, of Ian, their young son, of how his life and the quality therein contrasted with the 'no light at the end of the tunnel' meaningless and empty existence of the Sadie Kellys and the Nick McQueens of this world. He turned his collar up against the rain and walked to where he had parked the car. The car was a battered Ford and it was a pig to start in the damp. It fired on the fourth attempt. King gunned the engine and drove down through Kelvinbridge to Gibson Street and down Kelvin Way, passing the sad lonely boys hunching under umbrellas waiting for pick-up, each eyeing him hopefully as he swished past. It was at sudden, fleeting, times like this that he realized that he loved his wife, their child and their home very much indeed.

He parked the car at the rear of P Division police station and walked into the building by the rear 'Staff only' door. In the office that he shared with Montgomerie and the keen-as-mustard Abernethy, both at present out, he peeled off his raincoat, shaking the globules of moisture on to the carpet, and hung the dripping garment on a peg behind the door. He sat at his desk and read the notes that he had made before compiling his report. Only one point to bring out from his visit to Shane Dodemaide's twilight and under-privileged background: the manner of Shane Dodemaide's father's death and, following that, his mother impressing upon her children how to hold a knife by the handle with the blade upright and beside and behind them as they walked until it became second nature to them. Something in that, King thought, something very possibly relevant. Unknown to him, he was beginning to hone to perfection the policeman's facility that Fabian Donoghue privately referred to as his 'inner voice'. Don't ask where it comes from, don't question it, just listen to it. All good cops have it.

The same voice also told King that the mysterious Veronica might well be a stone worth turning over. She seemed a puzzling figure, coming in from nowhere in the deep mid-winter and leaving equally silently, just slipping away as the rain fell in springtime. She was apparently not involved in the murder of Eddie Wroe, having left the miserable squat before the murder had taken place, but she was known to both victim and accused, she had lived with both in every sense, probably was stolen by one from the other. No, he thought, no, probably she wasn't, probably she lived with both quite openly and Eddie Wroe and Shane Dodemaide both equally openly enjoyed the mysterious high-born Veronica, as she enjoyed their heroin in return. It was the way King had learned that smack-heads live: smack is the only currency.

He rose from his desk and went to the corner of the room and switched on the electric kettle. He made himself a mug of coffee and returned to his desk to write a full report, as full and well-rounded as possible and offering observations, with respect.

Montgomerie awoke. He awoke with a thick head, a head which in fact felt like a lump of lead and a throat which felt like the bottom of a birdcage. He turned to one side, towards the window of his bedroom. Outside it was dark and the rain streamed down the window-pane. Street lamps shimmered below his window and a bus hissed over the wet surface of the road. He glanced at the luminous dial of the clock on his bedside cabinet: 10.0 p.m. He had to be at work, on

80

duty, in one hour's time. He still wore his shirt, he had fallen asleep in the shirt that he had worn throughout the day. The rest of his clothing was strewn about the floor of his bedroom. He felt like a slob. He told himself that he was a slob, a slob who never ever seemed to learn from his own mistakes. You know the rules, Montgomerie, he said to himself, turning once again to look at the ceiling, you know them fine well. Lay off the alcohol when you are on night duty. It's a golden rule, pure solid gold. You come off duty at 7.0 a.m., don't hang around, straight home, straight into your pit, you know the routine, you can do it by numbers. Grab six hours of good nourishing alcohol-free sleep, wake up to enjoy the afternoon and evening, plenty to do, plenty to catch up on; if you've time on your hands you can always take in a film in the evening, but whatever you do, you start work refreshed and alert and sober at 11.0 p.m. Seven days in a row. Apart from anything else, think of the money you save and of the benefit to your liver.

Yet you do this. You fancy a pint and so you have one and then you get the taste and you keep drinking until you're legless and it's costing you money, it's costing you performance at work, it's costing you health, it's costing your self-esteem because here you are dragging yourself out of your pit when it's dark outside and it's wet outside and everybody else in the city is about to retire for the night and you are hung-over, at 10.0 p.m., staggering to the bathroom to brush your teeth, to make your mouth taste fresh and to hide your sour, stale breath; you are staggering to the kitchen to sink some coffee and groping open the fridge door to see if there's anything cold and quick to eat, because you can't face a big meal but you don't know what your body will be asked to do in the next eight hours so it must have fuel of some sort. Not that you have left yourself time to prepare a meal anyway, you've even left it too late to make up a packed meal for your little orange-coloured plastic lunch-box, a meal that you can eat with your feet up on the desk, killing time on the graveyard shift by reading someone else's newspaper or tackling the crossword that they couldn't finish.

You're a mess, Montgomerie. You're a pure mess.

He washed and pulled on a clean shirt, not his favourite shirt by any means, but it was the first one that came to hand. In the kitchen he was confronted by two days of washing-up. There was, though, a clean mug and an inch of coffee left in the jar. No milk, so he fell back on the powdered stuff. The result was a steamy mess with an interesting taste; not a bit like coffee but an interesting taste none the less. In the fridge he found some chicken pieces, some bread and some butter. The shopping that he had done that morning lay unpacked in two plastic bags leaning against the wall. At least he hadn't left them in the pub. He put the chicken pieces between two slices of buttered bread and began to eat. He pretended he was starving to death. It went down easier that way.

He returned to the bathroom and brushed his teeth again. Just to make sure his stale breath was killed outright. He combed his hair and slung on his jacket, checked that his wallet with his ID was still in the inside pocket, and glanced in the mirror. Well, he was still there, chiselled features, downturned moustache, dark thick head of hair, but he felt older than his twenty-seven years and his normal walk of long, effortless strides was on this occasion replaced by shaky, timid steps as he made his way down the common stair, into the close mouth, into the rain to where he had parked his car.

He drove cautiously, still feeling the residual effects of the day's intake of alcohol, chewing extra strong mints as he went. All that money just to dig a hole for yourself, it wasn't even an enjoyable drink, it was a good bucket right enough, but not enjoyable because you were by yourself, talking to yourself, inside your head, talking to yourself.

No, there was the merchant seaman. He remembered the merchant seaman; for a while they had talked to each other.

Malcolm, Malcolm.

Sitting in his car in a side street in Rutherglen listening to the rain pitter-patter on the roof, feeling the damp in his socks where his shoes had let in water and watching the

82

light from the bungalow shimmering through the drizzle, Detective-Sergeant Raymond Sussock, aged almost sixty years, having recently been granted an extension of service, gripped the steering-wheel and told himself that there was no road round it. No road at all.

He pulled on his gloves and twisted his trilby down tight around his lean skull and stepped out of the car. The rain fell vertically on his shoulders. He thrust his hands in his coat pockets, hunched up against the rain and walked towards the house lights that had once in his life been a welcome sight. He walked to the side door of the bungalow. He heard a television playing inside the house, the volume turned up much too loud. He knocked on the door and upon his knock the volume was turned down. A mellow male voice came to the door, too mellow in Sussock's opinion for the tender years of its owner. 'Who is it?'

'Me,' growled Sussock.

'Mummy, Mummy!' The voice behind the door rose to a near-hysterical scream. 'It's him. Daddy!'

Sussock heard a high-pitched scream from within the house. He hammered on the door.

'It's still him,' yelled Sussock, utterly unconcerned about the neighbours hearing the altercation. 'If he doesn't come through the door he can just as easily come through the window. You hear?!'

A bolt was drawn from behind the door and a chain fell away. The door opened. Samuel stood there, tall, slim, with rings in the lobes of each ear, a black pullover tucked into the waistband of his trousers, smooth hands rendered hairless by the use of the lotions on Mrs Sussock's dressing-table. 'Hello, Daddy,' he said, smiling.

Sussock pushed past him and was confronted by his wife. She was a small woman with a pinched face and glaring eyes.

She enjoyed hating. Sussock had realized that a long time ago.

He glared back at her.

'What do you want?' She spat the words at him.

He remained silent. Holding her stare, allowing her

hostility to wash over him, like a wave breaking around a rock. It was easy now, after all these years.

'What do you want?'

Sussock advanced on her.

'What do you want, what do you want, what do you want? Why come back here, why aren't you catching robbers? Never was any good, was he, Sammy?'

'Never, Mummy,' said Samuel, smiling as he looked on at the spectacle unfolding in the kitchen.

'Always out, out with his mates. Never here, not ever, was he, Sammy?'

'Never, Mummy.'

The shrew began to back up as Sussock advanced. She backed out of the kitchen, spitting words, like a cornered cat. She backed up the threshold of the living-room where she stood her ground. 'Not getting in here. Nothing of yours in here.'

Sussock walked past her down the hall and opened the door of a small box-room. He switched on the light and began to rummage through some cardboard boxes, collecting items of clothing as he did so, lighter summer clothing, a white raincoat which he enjoyed wearing. Then he walked back down the corridor, back to the kitchen, back towards the side door of the bungalow. Samuel sneered at him as he went past.

Sussock turned. 'Not be long now, son.'

'Not be long until what, Daddy, eh?'

'Till the divorce comes through, then I'll raise an action for Division and Sale and sell the property. Then you're on the street.'

'We'll survive, me and Mother,' said Samuel. 'Don't worry about us.'

'I don't,' said Sussock. 'Not any more. I wonder now why I ever did.'

The door was slammed shut behind him.

'Soon,' said the whimpering woman, 'soon, you can come into the house, maybe tomorrow. I spoke to Daddy. He's not a bad man. He says it's just like having 'flu. I brought you an extra blanket. He doesn't know that you've got it. He wouldn't want you to have it, but I know how cold it can get during the night.'

And the sweating, shivering young woman nodded as she clutched her stomach, accepting what was said to her, but complained that it wasn't like 'flu, not like having 'flu at all, she couldn't say what it was like but it was ten times worse than anything you could imagine, and if it was hysterical why were the cramps so intense and why did the bones ache so much, and if it was hysterical why were her clothes and her sheets damp with sweat? That wasn't hysteria.

'But Daddy says it is.' The woman wrapped her arms around her daughter. 'Grit your teeth. If you scream and shout again you'll have to stay here. You'll never get back in the house. I'm going now. I'll turn the light off. Good night.'

Elka Willems signed off at 11.0 p.m. She drove home to Langside, to her home, just a room and kitchen which she had decorated in pastel shades and a Van Gogh print on the wall adjacent to the bed. She parked her car and entered the close and walked up the common stair and enjoyed the smell of disinfectant which assailed her. There was nothing more pleasing than a clean stair. She turned the stair and saw her landing and saw him standing there, dripping, a parcel of clothing in his arms. His thin, craggy face cracked into a smile. She paused and returned the smile and then walked up the stair and stood in front of him. She kissed him. 'Been here long?'

'About half an hour,' he said. Nearer two was more accurate.

'Poor old Sussock,' she said. 'Dear poor old Sussock.' She turned the key in the lock of the door of her flat.

85

CHAPTER 6

Tuesday, 21.10–Wednesday 13.00 hours

Even then it was a dog of a shift: a real bitch.

He found Richard King waiting in the CID room, hat and coat on, ready to depart. King looked disapprovingly at him as he entered the room.

'So I'm late.' Montgomerie peeled off his yellow and blue ski jacket. 'Ten minutes. I mean, what's ten minutes?'

'Nothing compared to your breath, my son.' King rose from his seat. 'Been on the batter, have we?'

'Yes, "we" have. Is it that bad?'

'It's like a flame-thrower.'

'And I've been chewing strong mints like there's no tomorrow.'

'And that's also what I can smell, even from here. There's only one reason why a guy would eat mints in that quantity. I mean, you may as well let them smell the hot breath of the really crucial bevvy merchant without adulterating it with mint.'

Montgomerie sank into the chair in front of his desk with clumsy uncoordinated movements.

'Talk about bleary-eyed!' said King. 'Bloodshot, more like!'

'Give it a rest, will you?' Montgomerie laid his head in his hands. 'It's just one of those things. Make me a cup of coffee, will you?'

'No.' King buttoned his coat.

'Cup of coffee for a dying soldier?'

'No. I'm going home.'

'You're all heart, you know that?'

'Yes, and it belongs at home with wife and child, my son, and it's not to be used for propping up derelicts like you. You'll be pleased to know that there's nothing to hand over.'

'Nothing?'

'Not a thing, nothing lying in anticipation of your individual attention. The city sleeps. You might be able to do the same with a bit of luck.'

Richard King left the room and Montgomerie sat in silence.

The city was sleeping. 'Hush! Whisper who dares,' said Montgomerie to himself as he rose from his seat and cautiously made himself a mug of coffee. He knew this city, this red-haired Irish bitch of a city, with her two long legs straddling the Clyde and meeting at the intimacy of the grid system at her centre; this bitch didn't really sleep, she slumbered perhaps, but slumbered with one eye open ready to rise up. Snarling.

And she did just that at 23.41 according to the CID log, just as Montgomerie had started on his third mug of coffee.

The phone on his desk rang. He glared at it for a second and then reluctantly took his feet off the desktop, reached for his notebook and pen, picked up the receiver and said, 'CID.'

'Uniform bar, sir,' said the voice on the phone. 'CID attendance requested by Tango Delta Foxtrot. They're at the GRI Casualty. Involves a mugging.'

'On my way.' Montgomerie put the phone down, grabbed his coat, slid another mint between his teeth and chomped it in two, despite King's opinion on the matter. He drove across Glasgow. Street lights shimmered in the rain and glistened on the wet road surface. The streets were heavy with late night traffic, but the pavements were empty, mostly. Just a group of women on heels and under umbrellas, talking on a corner; a few men, collars turned against the rain; a few drunks too legless even to notice the rain.

At the Casualty Department of the GRI a young-looking doctor with a university tie and a white coat said, 'Two old ladies. One has been sent to theatre, she has multiple fractures, the other is in here. She has shock.'

'Are the injuries serious?'

'At their time of life they are potentially fatal; even the

lady who is just in a state of shock.' The doctor thrust his hands deep into the pocket of his coat.

A scream suddenly pierced the Casualty ward. Montgomerie glanced up.

'Fellow ran into a plate glass window,' said the doctor. 'Ran, or was pushed. Anyway, he's lucky to be alive, no major organs or arteries penetrated, but he's a shrapnel job from top to toe and it's all got to be pulled out, sliver by sliver, and some of them are four or five inches long.'

'Painful.'

'Very—and slow. Can't snap the glass when extracting it, and it's got to be a meticulous square inch by square inch search of his flesh because glass will not show up on X-ray. I put two experienced nurses on the job. It will probably take them most of the night.'

'I'll need to be careful where I step.'

'Just another Tuesday, going into Wednesday,' said the doctor, and Montgomerie realized that the man's apparent youth belied the hard-bitten cynicism of a veteran.

'Well, the old ladies. One, as I said, is in theatre. The other lady is fit to be discharged, but she's in such a state of shock that she can't go home because I'm pretty certain that more shock will set in soon and at a deeper level. I've given her a mild sedative but she's not strong enough to be fully sedated; that could kill her. I've contacted the Welfare Services and they are going to admit her to an aged persons' home for a few nights. That way she'll be supervised and somebody will be on hand if she does go into shock again.'

'Can I speak to her?'

'Behind the curtain.' The doctor nodded to a cubicle behind and to the left of him.

'Miss,' said the silver-haired lady, correcting Montgomerie and speaking in the soft lilting accent of a native of Skye. 'We are both "Miss", me and my sister. We never married.'

'I'm sorry.'

The elderly lady smiled. She had a glazed look in her eyes. She seemed to know where she was but Montgomerie detected a sense of dreamlike detachment about her perception of the present. Montgomerie recognized shock. He'd been there himself a couple of times, once in uniform and once in plain clothes.

'How's my sister?'

'She has broken bones.'

'That could be dangerous. I am eighty. She is seventy-seven. At our age, bones are brittle.'

'I know. Can you tell me what happened?'

'We were hit from behind and knocked to the ground. We were walking home from the prayer meeting. We are members of the Free Presbyterian Church, you see. We were walking home across the bridge—you know, the footbridge at Charing Cross—and we were hit from behind. Sarah was knocked to the ground and her handbag was snatched. I was pushed to the railings and then I fell, but I hung on to my bag and they ran away.'

'They?'

'There were two, two of them.'

'Did you see them?'

Miss McDonald shook her head. 'I don't see very well at the best of times. It was dark and it was raining. I couldn't even tell if they were men or women. They didn't speak, but they were young. They ran away very quickly.'

Montgomerie's jaw began to tighten. A cold anger rose in him.

'I hurt myself as I fell and I couldn't get up. I crawled over to where Sarah was and I saw that she was hurt. I crawled on to the end of the bridge and a good Samaritan was passing and he summoned the police.'

'How much money was in your sister's purse?'

'About four pounds.' She spoke in a calm and deferential manner. 'How long will I be here? I'd like to go home.'

'The hospital has made arrangements for you to spend some time in an old people's home. They would like someone to keep an eye on you. You're still in a state of shock.'

'If they think that that is for the best.'

Montgomerie went to the locus of the offence. The foot-bridge formed a high arch over the two lanes of traffic at Charing Cross. It was narrow, had railings at either side;

there was no room to manœuvre. It was the sort of route in mid-city that streetwise young women avoid for the very reason that two elderly spinsters were at present in the GRI. The bridge is convenient, very convenient in an ideal world, but in the real world it offers no escape from violent attack and for that reason and that reason alone, Montgomerie held, not many people use it after dark. He stood on the summit of the bridge and watched the cars swish beneath him and felt and heard the rain patter on the back of his jacket. He thought that the elderly Misses McDonald really had had no choice; they could hobble across the street clutching each other and perhaps make it to the far side, by hopping roundabouts, without getting flattened by a taxi, or they could hobble across the footbridge and perhaps make it without getting flattened by muggers. They had, he thought, probably done the journey between the Tabernacle and their home via the footbridge hundreds of times but eventually it had to happen, even in this city that is as safe as any other city and a far sight safer than most, despite its reputation; eventually they would be rolled by muggers. Most probably smack-heads desperate for money for more poison.

Even Montgomerie, with his cynicism and his years of police work, couldn't believe that people would do this sort of thing for kicks.

He walked to the Woodlands Road end of the bridge. Two beat cops stood, their capes dripping with the rain. One cop walked along the shrub line, shining his torch amid the branches as he went, the other examined a handbag. As Montgomerie approached, he recognized the officer who was examining the handbag to be Phil Hamilton, a good man, a little pedestrian, but very thorough; a man who wrote 'how, why, what, when, where and who' on the first page of each new notebook, twenty-four years old, married to a nurse, or so Montgomerie understood.

'Just about to bring this up to you, sir.' Hamilton looked up as Montgomerie approached. Montgomerie took the bag as Hamilton offered it to him. It was an old bag of good quality leather, with a velvet lining which was torn in places.

It contained a prayer book inside which was written the name and address of the lady who was presently in the operating theatre of the GRI. There was a comb, a handkerchief and nothing else. The purse and the princely sum of four pounds that it contained and any allowance book had been taken. He handed the bag back to Hamilton.

'Found anything else?'

'Not a thing, sir.'

'Well, get this in a plastic bag, tag it and get it to Forensic as soon as you can. They might be able to lift prints, but I doubt it somehow. Too much moisture about.'

Montgomerie walked up Woodlands Road, car showrooms, antique shops, Asian video rental shops, kebab shops, dark empty closes, tenements with a few showing lights. He walked on to the forecourt of the all-night service station. It was busy, cars queued up at the pumps. He went to the kiosk and spoke through the grille to a tall, thin, bearded man who wore a black baseball cap. He asked the man if he'd seen anything suspicious. 'About an hour ago, two people, young.'

The tall, thin man shook his head. 'I'd like to help you, sir,' he said, 'but young people, old people, middle-aged people, all stop here, not just motorists; pedestrians, people on the road home from the town, stop off to buy cigarettes, a can of juice, chocolate. Didn't notice anything out of the ordinary. No one excited or agitated.'

'Well, thanks anyway,' said Montgomerie. 'A packet of mints, please.'

Montgomerie drove back to P Division. He drank more coffee, wrote up the McDonald case, gave it an identification number. He drank more coffee and then the phone rang.

'Code 7, sir,' said the voice on the other end of the line; and seemed to Montgomerie apologetic in tone.

'Details, please.'

The details took him to a large house in Hyndland and the owner of same who was shaking with rage. Montgomerie had to concede that as Code 7's go, this was a particularly bad incident. The thieves had gained access by smashing a

91

pane of an irreplaceable stained glass window at the front of the house, had stolen expensive items of jewellery, clothing; they had of course stolen the video recorder and sundry other items such as cameras. They had left the house via the rear garden and had escaped the area by taking a little used access road which ran the length of the terrace. They had then apparently returned and systematically desecrated the property. They had spray-painted the walls, carved deep grooves on valuable furniture, kicked in glass panels, tipped the goldfish on to the floor, wrung the neck of the budgerigar and left the cat quaking with fear on the top shelf of the bookcase.

'I've been violated, violated,' said the man, shaking with rage. 'Violated.'

Montgomerie left a card giving his name and his office telephone number and requested that the police be informed of any suspicious sightings. He told the householder that a representative of the Forensic Department would visit later, during office hours, to dust for fingerprints.

'They left this behind them.' The man pointed to a rolled-up newspaper.

'Certain it's not yours?'

'Certain.'

'They probably used it to cushion themselves against the glass when they broke in. I'll take it with me.' Montgomerie held the paper delicately. 'It's what we call alien to the locus and it may contain prints.'

'You can lift fingerprints from paper?' The man seemed to be calming and began to show a keen interest in police procedure.

'Yes. It's difficult and takes time, but it's not impossible. It's done by a method known as the anhydrant process.'

'Bloody animals.'

It was Wednesday, 01.45.

More mints. More coffee. Another case written up, another case given an identification number. A case file to be dropped into Detective-Inspector Donoghue's in-tray to await attention during the working day. More coffee.

The shift had been dross up to that point. All dross. The

two old ladies wouldn't think that they were dross and Montgomerie himself didn't think that the incident was dross, and the home-owner who had been violated wouldn't think that his case was dross, but if crime ranges from littering on one hand to genocide on the other, then the bulk of cases on that shift had been closer to littering than they were to mass murder.

Not so the next incident. It was not a crime as such but it was an incident of behaviour which reached Montgomerie and was to stay with him for many, many years.

He arrived when the smell of roast meat was fresh and hung strongly in the living-room and the woman sat sobbing on the sofa. Earlier she had been hysterical, now she was only sobbing and was able to describe the human torch dancing round the coffee table.

'I said he'd stolen the Giro cheque,' sobbed the woman, little more than a girl. 'He said he hadn't; I said he had; he said he hadn't; I said he had and he had to go, we're not married, see. This is my house and I said that he'd have to go, so he said he wasn't going and he fetched a bottle of paraffin from the kitchen, a big bottle, and he poured it over himself and he got the cigarette lighter my sister brought me back from Malta last year and he flicked it . . . held it close and flicked it . . . I ran for the neighbour, she's got a phone. I phoned the police and he was still standing when the police came. Earlier he'd been dancing round the coffee table, slow like, all flames; when the police arrived he'd stopped and was standing still . . . and will you look at my ceiling?'

The beat cops had shoulder-charged the man, knocked him to the floor, smothered the flames with their capes and taken him to the Western Infirmary in the police vehicle. Montgomerie called at the hospital and was shown a body swathed in tinfoil with a small breathing hole for the mouth and small slits for the eyes.

'We'll do what we can for him.' The strikingly attractive female doctor's eyes widened as she gazed at Montgomerie's chiselled features, his downturned moustache and thick black hair, as in fact he had noticed women gaze at him since he was seventeen. 'But if he survives, he might not thank us; he has third degree burns over ninety per cent of his body. If he survives he'll only be able to sweat from his scalp and his feet. The rest of him is done to a turn.'

'Even his face.'

'Especially his face. It'll take years to reconstruct a recognizable face. Or perhaps I should say a face that's recognizable as human. Right now it looks a bit like a stuffed pepper straight out of the oven. What happened?'

Montgomerie told her.

'Stupid, stupid, stupid,' said the doctor. 'What has he proved?'

'What do any of them prove?'

'And it's so selfish. I wouldn't have minded if he had been injured in an accident, but the National Health Service is bankrupt, he is going to cost us thousands and thousands to repair, and it was all avoidable because it was self-induced. All this because he wanted to prove a point to his lady-friend.'

03.21 hours. The shift was dragging in.

The young woman stood, naked, in her kitchen in her flat in Langside, letting the soft light from the hall illuminate the room, the sink, the pearl grey working surface, the table, the shower cubicle. She cupped both hands around the glass of milk and stared out of the window, at the rain running down the glass and the light burning in the house opposite across the far side of the black back court. She moved her head and her lemon hair wafted across her shoulders. She stepped backwards with a lightness of step and leaned against the table, the edge of the table nestling against the lower curve of her buttocks. She sipped the milk until the glass was empty and, setting the glass silently on the table behind her, returned to the bedroom, walking on tiptoe across the deep pile carpet, slid under the duvet and placed her arm around the man.

The man grunted.

'Sorry, did I wake you?' whispered the woman. 'Sorry.'

94

'No,' the man murmured. 'I was awake when you got up. Can't seem to sleep.'

'Nor can I.'

'What time is it?'

'Three-thirty.'

'Still raining?' asked Ray Sussock.

'Still raining,' said Elka Willems.

Ink-black night in the city of Glasgow and still the rain fell vertically in the calm, cold April air. Montgomerie was diverted by radio to a Code 41. Like most Code 41s in his experience, he found it bloody, cheap, grubby and senseless. By the time Montgomerie arrived at the top flat of the dirty close in Priesthill, the corpse had been removed by the ambulance crew and the assailant sat, open-eyed and ashen-faced, handcuffed to a uniformed officer. The assailant was a young man of twenty, the victim was younger; the murder weapon was an ice-pick and was sticky with congealed blood inside a plastic bag in the rear of the police car. Upstairs was the widow of the murdered man, nineteen years of age, with an infant son.

'What's the story?' Montgomerie asked of the second beat cop who stood in the corner of the room, allowing the bumbling, clumsy thick-lensed, spectacled Elliot Bothwell, forensic chemist, to photograph the locus. There was no need for him to dust for prints on this occasion.

'Gentleman on the settee, he was carrying on a liaison with the lady. The deceased, the lady's husband, came home . . .'

Montgomerie groaned. 'I see,' he said.

'It was self-defence,' said the young man on the couch. He spoke with a timid, frightened voice. 'He was going to knife me.'

'Take him down to the police station, please,' said Montgomerie. 'I'll speak to him there.'

Montgomerie knew what would happen. He would charge the man with murder; the man's lawyer would plea-bargain guilty of culpable homicide, didn't intend to kill, plea accepted, given a five-year stretch in the slammer, out in three.

Just in time to see the murdered man's child start nursery school and he would henceforth be revered on the scheme as a 'hard man'.

Montgomerie left the flat and went down the common stair, stood in the close mouth and glanced at the hard man with a small face, a ned who'd got hold of an ice-pick and dislodged another young man's brains from his skull. The preliminary report from the pathology laboratory would indicate the deepest and most damaging blows had been struck from behind. Some hard man. Some self-defence.

Montgomerie looked up. Dawn was beginning to break, a crack of grey to the south, just below the blackness. The birds didn't sing. He noticed that before. No dawn chorus if it is raining.

He drove back to P Division. No messages in his pigeon-hole. He drank a mug of coffee and decided to let the hard man from Priesthill sweat a little. It was 05.35.

Two hours later he handed over the shift to Ray Sussock. Sussock, who had slumbered after being woken in the middle of the night, re-awoke refreshed and rested. He breakfasted with Elka Willems, hurriedly but not under pressure, he in his clothing, she in a full-length yellow towelling robe. He had a second cup of coffee while he waited for her to dress in her uniform of unflattering serge and do her hair up into a tight bun behind her head. She put on her chequered white and black cravat which was fixed at the nape of her neck by a strip of adhesive and would therefore come away easily in the hands of anyone who tried to garotte her with it. She put on her hat and twisted it on to her head and re-appeared in the kitchen; to Sussock, she looked just as breathtakingly beautiful as when she had tiptoed across the carpet, naked, a few hours earlier. They left the flat together and drove across the city to Charing Cross in the centre of town, Sussock dropping her off to walk the last half-mile to the police station itself. Sussock parked his car in the car park at the rear of the police station, and entered the building. He went to his office and peeled off his trench coat

96

and battered trilby and left his office to go in search of Malcolm Montgomerie. It was 06.38.

Sussock found Montgomerie, feet on his desk, arms folded on his chest, head down and snoring fit to drive the cattle home.

''Morning, Malcolm,' Sussock said loudly.

Montgomerie continued to snore.

Sussock lifted Montgomerie's feet off the desk and shook his shoulder. 'Come on, look alive!'

Montgomerie shook himself awake and squeezed his eyes. 'Sorry, Sarge, I guess I nodded off.'

'I guess you did. Good job I found you and not Fabian.' Sussock turned and walked out of the room. 'My office in fifteen minutes. Give you time to wash the sleep from your eyes and throw some coffee down your throat.'

Coffee, thought Sussock walking down the corridor to his office, now there's a good idea if ever there was one. He turned into his office and walked to the window, where his locker stood. He opened his locker, took out his mug and glanced out of the window. Elka Willems was walking smartly and briskly towards the police station in good time for muster at 07.10. She was not and never had been one of the stragglers who came panting into the muster room full of apologies as the duty watch was falling in.

Sussock mixed instant coffee with powdered milk, went to the CID rest-room and poured boiling water from the geyser into the mug, stirring the mixture as he did so; the end result at least bore a passing resemblance to coffee. Sussock sat away from the window, observing the directive of Chief Superintendent Findlater that it does not look well for officers to be seen sitting or standing by the window drinking coffee. He scanned the early edition of the *Herald* which had been left in the rest-room and sipped the contents of his mug, which had a sufficiently coffee-like taste to warrant a second mugful. This he took to his office to await Montgomerie's arrival.

Sussock addressed himself to the *Herald* crossword, cracked two down, which led neatly into four across, just as

97

Montgomerie tapped on his door, carrying an armful of files in one hand and a mug of coffee in the other.

'Take a pew.' Sussock folded up the paper and placed it to one side of his desk. Montgomerie lowered himself into the chair which stood in front of Sussock's desk.

'So-so,' he said, 'it was so-so.'

'Let's hear it.'

'One murder,' said Montgomerie.

'Only one?'

'Messy. It's the old, old story. Husband comes home and finds another man carrying on with his old lady. There's a rammy and the husband gets an ice-pick buried in his skull. The way I'm talking you'd think they were adults, but they're little more than children. Late teens, early twenties. The killer is claiming self-defence, but the pathologist informed us that many of the blows and certainly the fatal one fell on the back of the victim's skull. I think he's got some explaining to do, but anyway he's downstairs, cautioned and charged.

'Old story, as you say.'

'One stolen Giro cheque.'

'Malcolm, I'll thank you not to try my patience with trivia!'

'Well, it is a reported theft,' said Montgomerie, in his own defence, and went on to tell Sussock about the man in the Western Infirmary, wrapped in tinfoil with slits for eyes and mouth and drips in his arm.

'God in Heaven,' said Sussock.

'Thought it would brighten up your morning, Sarge.' Montgomerie smiled. 'The man's lady-friend whose Giro it was seemed to be more concerned about her ceiling. It's covered in a layer of reddish-looking fat.' Montgomerie handed the file to Sussock.

'Next is a burglary, theft and damage. You know the scene—spray-painted the walls, urinated and defecated everywhere. Quite a big team, going by the damage, and a nasty job. I've sent the report of the M.O. to the Collator to see if he can tie it up with any other similar burglaries or known felons who do this sort of thing. I've left word with Forensic, asking them to visit to dust for prints.'

'Right,' said Sussock, 'we'll leave that on one side until we get word from Forensic and the Collator.'

'Finally, a mugging.' Montgomerie handed the last file to Sussock and spoke from memory. 'Two old ladies on their way back from a Bible study group; they got rolled, right outside our front door, in fact, as they were crossing the footbridge at Charing Cross.'

'Lost much?'

'Lost their confidence ever to go out at night again, but in terms of hard cash, just four pounds, which is more to them than it is to either you or me. One lady—they're sisters—one lady is badly shaken and the Welfare people are looking after her. The other has broken bones, which at her advanced years could prove to be fatal.'

'Could be murder?'

'Be worth a try if she croaks. We got a murder conviction on those two neds who broke into the old lady's house and so frightened her that it induced a heart attack.'

'Yes. We also lost it when they appealed against the conviction. But, as you say, if a causal link can be established, then it's worth it. Make them sweat for a week or two before the trial, at least. They'll think twice before mugging a pensioner again.'

'That's only if we catch 'em. Talking of old stories, it's the one you've heard before—no witnesses, no identification other than that they were young and that there were two of them.'

'Be druggies, I guess.'

'Well, again it's down to Forensic. We found the handbag—it was discarded after it had been rifled; if Forensic can lift any prints, we're up and running. We get to know all the druggies sooner or later and they're all equally careless.'

Sussock grunted.

'Well, that's me, Sarge.' Montgomerie stood. 'I'll sign off now, if there's nothing else.'

*

The girl lay on the bed. She stared out of the bolted-down window at the low grey clouds scudding over the hill, heavy with rain. Her body was racked with pain, like drills; she closed her eyes and imagined drills, not just small dentists' drills but big masonry drills or slowly turning carpenters' drills, grinding into the joints of her limbs, her shoulders, her elbows, her knees, her ankles, and the cramps in her stomach gripping, easing off, gripping again. She turned and buried her face in the pillow and felt the moisture of her brow as it came into contact with the pillowcase, and the moisture of the bed linen dampened with the endless perspiration which pumped out of her pores. Beside the bed was the bowl and in the bowl was vomit, her vomit. It wasn't proper vomit, not healthy substantial vomit in which can be recognized half-digested food; it was all liquid, colourless, a little gelatinous, but almost wholly clear liquid, being the water she had consumed but couldn't retain. She had drunk it the previous evening, two bottles of mineral water, to counteract the sweating and it had come back on her at intervals during the night. She tossed and turned, tried to keep it down, but eventually it had come up her gullet; clear water, mostly.

She turned back from the pillow and looked up at the grey sky and the dawning of another day. Her long black hair lay pushed up over the back of the pillow behind her head. She kept it there, out of the way; she didn't want puke in it.

Another hour, maybe. The girl looked at the clock beside her bed. 07.30. Yes, about another hour and she'll come in, opening the door with a blast of cold air. They didn't need to lock her in, the cold air and lack of clothing kept her near the radiator. She'll come in—an innocent flat round face which always reminded the girl of faces in mediæval tapestries. She even had the page-boy hairstyle to set it off, but she was too old, this woman, to make the page-boy style look fetching and she just looked prim. She was prim; that's why she looked prim, in a cotton dress and a cardigan and flat shoes over thick tights, and concerned eyes. She probably was concerned, but if she had only stood up to

100

him or had stepped in when she was standing up to him instead of cringing there, whimpering in the corner, wringing her hands while the words flew backwards and forwards prior to the blows flying in one direction . . . if only she had stood up to him, then she herself would not be lying here in this wooden torture chamber. Soon she would come in, gently peeking her head round the door as though she was visiting a patient in hospital, only she wouldn't be carrying flowers or a bag of grapes, but a tray of food, poached egg on toast—'Here we are, dear, your favourite; and the paper—the Woman's *Herald* is good today.'

Poached eggs on toast, her favourite. The girl looked up at the wooden beams above her head and smelled the creosote as she breathed in through her nose, fighting a sudden cramp in her stomach, her stomach which would soon be in receipt of a poached egg on a slice of toast, her favourite meal, being the only meal she could keep down. And a mug of tea, don't forget the tea.

Montgomerie didn't feel tired, possibly because he had slept a little towards the end of the shift, possibly because he had slept late the previous day and by the time he signed off duty at 08.00, he had been awake for less than ten hours. He returned to his flat and picked up the mail; two bills and a circular. One bill from the Gas Board was red; he laid that on one side. The other, from the South of Scotland Electricity Board, was blue. He tossed it contemptuously into the waste-bin along with the circular. He washed, changed his shirt, hustled a hot breakfast, two rashers of bacon, well past their 'sell by' date and a can of beans.

More coffee.

The incident of the two elderly sisters mugged for four pounds had reached him. He was not often affected by incidents, but that one had reached home. He sat sipping the coffee and listened to the radio, waiting until the clock ticked round to 11.00 and opening time. At five to eleven he left his flat just off Highburgh Road and drove across the city to the Round Toll. He parked the car next to a patch

101

of waste ground and went into a bar called the Gay Gordon.

There were not, in Montgomerie's experience, many bars like the Gay Gordon left in the city. Just one room, standing on the junction of two roads; once there were tenements about it; the tenements had been torn down and just the bar was left, a pillbox of a building on the corner of an expanse of waste ground, all rubbish tips and marram grass, 'awaiting development'. Inside the Gay Gordon, the horsehair had been pulled out of upholstery and the stools and tables were fastened to the floor with chains as much to prevent them from being liberated for use as household furnishings as to prevent them being used as weapons in the inevitable Friday-night rammy. The television set, fastened high up on the wall, with both the volume and colour turned up too loudly, beamed in a picture from another planet; a horse being led around a paddock in an English shire, prior to racing.

Tuesday Noon sat in the far corner of the room beneath the television set. He nodded as Montgomerie entered the bar. Montgomerie walked across the sawdust to the gantry and ordered a double whisky and a soda water with lime, heavy on the lime. He took the drink and walked across to where Tuesday Noon was sitting and sat opposite him. The older man took the whisky, drank it down neat in one go and rasped hot breath across the table at Montgomerie.

'Christ, Tuesday! It's not even midday yet.'

Montgomerie drank the soda and lime.

Tuesday Noon grinned, a red face of whiskies and matted silver silver hair, a black mouth with a few yellow pegs going up and down.

'And it's time for your annual bath, Tuesday.' Montgomerie cradled the glass in his lap. 'Maybe I should just take you in on all those outstanding warrants for all those unpaid fines, get you cleaned up and your clothes de-loused. As it is, you're a hazard to public health. You could do with the doctor's needle in your backside again. When did you last get your protein fix? More than a year since you've been in the slammer, isn't it? I'm being too good to you, Tuesday, far too good.'

102

Tuesday Noon pushed the glass across the table towards Montgomerie and grinned a near-toothless grin.

'You know the rules, Tuesday. You get a drink if and when I get a result. Mind you, you can have this soda and lime if you want. I don't want it.'

Tuesday Noon sat back against the bench.

'Tuesday, last night when you and all other good men and true were safe abed, two neds rolled two old ladies for the princely sum of four quid. That's about one-tenth of what it would take to get you good and drunk. And it's about one-tenth of what I'll give you if you can point me in the direction of said neds. One old lady is in hospital with broken bones, the other is in a home in a state of shock. I want the men who did it.'

Tuesday Noon nodded. He said he'd keep his eyes and ears open.

'Oh, do more than that, Tuesday. Start sniffing around, start hunting.'

'All right, Mr Montgomerie.'

Montgomerie stood. 'It's not a serious crime as crimes go, but on this occasion, like I said, there's a good drink in it for you if you come up with the goods.'

'All right, Mr Montgomerie.'

Montgomerie turned to leave the bar.

'Oh, Mr Montgomerie . . .'

'What is it, Tuesday?'

'Don't suppose you'll be interested, but I saw Mr Bentley in his Bentley on Sunday morning.'

'So who he and what of he?'

'He's a solicitor. He instructed my defence counsel when I went down for that five-year stretch.'

'No wonder you recognized him.'

'Well, he was tearing down Bath Street in his big blue Bentley, Mr Bentley in a Bentley.'

'So?'

'At about six in the morning. I mean burning rubber, shooting red lights.'

Montgomerie shrugged. 'Don't read into things, Tuesday, such habits are dangerous. He probably just wanted to get home before his lady wife woke up to find that he'd been out on the ran-dan all night.'

Only when he was home and climbing into his bed did Montgomerie wonder that Tuesday Noon was doing in Bath Street at 6.0 a.m. on Sunday morning.

CHAPTER 7

Wednesday, 13.00–1730 hours

Donoghue reached forward and picked up the tall silver coffee-pot which stood on the table in the centre of Findlater's office. He replenished his cup and replaced the pot on the table. Donoghue longed to draw out his pipe, but Findlater was the Chief Superintendent and so the boss; Findlater didn't approve of smoking in his office. He also said that his plants didn't like it. He possessed two huge rubber plants, one at either side of the office window, and since the Chief Superintendent had on occasions been found chatting amicably to the said vegetables, then Donoghue reasoned the plants' wishes as well as the Chief Superintendent's had most certainly to be respected.

Findlater was a huge man who moved softly and easily; likewise he replenished his cup and relaxed back into the easy chair. Findlater had risen from the rank of constable in his native Elgin to Chief Superintendent in Glasgow within a respectable thirty years of unblemished and uninterrupted service. He had by then turned his office into a den; there were the plants, there was a photograph of the upper reaches of the Tay and a second photograph showing the Chief Superintendent in a felt hat, casting a fly over a Borders stream. He was a contented man, sliding gently towards retirement.

'So it's not so open and shut then, Fabian?'

'Not a bit of it, sir.' Donoghue sipped his coffee. 'The young man was found murdered on Sunday morning, three

104

mornings ago. A knife, which could have been the murder weapon and which could as easily not have been, was found near the body. Fingerprints lifted from the knife belonged to a known petty felon who was a mate of the deceased. They lived in the same miserable squat, shared a girl and probably shared each other's works as well.'

'Ah yes, both were heroin addicts. Up to this point, it did appear to be open and shut.'

'So we thought at the time, sir.'

'Then things became muddier?'

'To say the least, sir. Dr Reynolds pointed out that the deceased, Eddie Wroe, had been murdered elsewhere. His body had lain face up until rigor had set in. The rigor was then broken and the body moved, probably to where it was found. Death was due to stabbing and the wounds could have been made by the knife found by the body, which was covered in the deceased's blood, incidentally.'

'Incidentally.' Findlater glanced lovingly at his rubber plants. 'So if the murderer dumped both the body and the knife with Shane—what's his name . . .?'

'Dodemaide,' said Donoghue, 'Shane Dodemaide.'

'Yes, Dodemaide, then if the body and the knife had Dodemaide's prints on it, then such an act could only have been done to implicate Dodemaide and throw us off the scent.

'My reasoning exactly, sir.'

'And I noted when reading the file that Dr Kay's findings tie in neatly with Dr Reynolds's.'

'Yes, sir. Dr Kay was able to inform us that the body lay on a greasy, oily surface and suggested, for example, the floor of a garage.'

'Anything of interest in their—er—home?'

'Only their lady-friend, sir, present whereabouts unknown. She apparently moved in to the squat right out of the blue, stayed for a few weeks and left equally neatly. Our inquiries indicate her name to be Veronica . . . and her background somewhat privileged.'

'You're searching for her?'

'Yes, sir. I feel that she's a stone that will be worth turning over. In fact, I've got Abernethy working on it right now. Shouldn't take him too long. Just two phone calls, in fact. We understand her to have been a law student at one of the universities. She must have "dropped out", as I understand the term to be, from any one of four years' intake of students at either university.'

'Two phone calls, as you say. Are you missing a female student called Veronica?'

'Who is tall and dark-haired,' said Donoghue. 'That's the description we have been given.'

'Shouldn't be too difficult. What else do you intend to do?'

'I'd like to drive out to see Shane Dodemaide. He's been remanded on a murder charge for forty-eight hours now; should have focused his thoughts nicely. I'd like to see what he has to say about the matter.'

Abernethy read over the report and thought it satisfactory. It was full without being long-winded, he'd put himself into it, offered reasoned and qualified opinion and observation, but had made no judgement. Yes, he was not displeased with it. He signed it and left his desk and walked down the CID corridor to DI Donoghue's office. He found the door open and the office empty. He entered and slid his report into Donoghue's in-tray. He turned.

Donoghue stood in the doorway. 'Yes, Abernethy?' He had a number of files under his arm.

'The report on the suicide, sir,' Abernethy stammered. He was youthful, uncertain, still in his early twenties, very, very young for a plain clothes officer, but the potential was all there, at least to Donoghue's eyes and evidently to the eyes of the promotion board as well.

'Ah yes, I'll glance over it, but in future, take anything for my attention downstairs and leave it in my pigeonhole. I know it's convenient to walk along the corridor and pop it into my in-tray, but it's a little undiplomatic. I control what goes into my in-tray. That's the way it works.'

'I'm sorry, sir.'

Donoghue walked past Abernethy and dropped the files

on his desktop. He reached hungrily for his pipe. 'Any word from the universities on the girl?' He played the flame of the cigarette lighter over the pipe bowl, sucking and blowing as he did so.

'Not yet, sir, I don't think that they'll be too long. I emphasized that it was a murder inquiry.'

'Good.' Donoghue settled into his chair, enjoying the pipe. 'If you'd let me know as soon as you hear anything.'

'Yes, sir.' Abernethy walked back down the CID corridor to the detective-constables' room. The phone on his desk was ringing. He picked it up. 'Abernethy,' he said.

'Glasgow University holding for you, sir,' said the controller's voice.

'Oh yes.'

'Law Faculty, Glasgow, here,' said an efficient female voice. 'I hope you don't mind us calling you back, but we had to be sure that it was the police to whom we are giving the information.'

'Of course,' said Abernethy, 'we're anxious to trace this young lady.'

'So are we.'

'Oh?'

'Yes. We have actually reported her to the police as a missing person. The police followed up by visiting her home address and we got a flea in our ear from her irate father— we had no right to report her missing without consulting him. Actually we did both at the same time, told the police and informed him.'

'You didn't check that she hadn't returned home?'

'We did. In fact, I made the call. Spoke to Veronica's mother. She said that Veronica wasn't at home, by which she meant that Veronica hadn't returned home. So on that basis, we alerted the police. The lady sounded a little timid and indecisive, but she certainly told her husband because he came on the phone a few minutes later, phoning from his place of work, roaring like a bear with a sore head. He didn't seem so concerned about his daughter so much as he was furiously indignant that we hadn't consulted him. But we had consulted one of the parents—that was enough for us.'

'So who is she?'

'Girl called Veronica Bentley.'

Abernethy held the phone between his ear and shoulder as he scribbled on his pad.

'She was, still is, I hope, a second-year student, twenty years old. She apparently did a very good first year but then seemed to lose all interest and confidence. She lost all motivation, neglected her appearance, stopped attending lectures, tutorial attendance became worryingly infrequent, until finally she was noticeable only by her absence. We inquired of her friends but they knew nothing of her whereabouts. She had vanished.'

'When was that?'

'Just after Christmas.' The voice faltered. 'Wait a minute. I have her file here. Yes, we reported her as missing on the twenty-first of January. She hadn't been seen for three days prior to that. She is still missing so far as we know.'

'I see.' Abernethy continued to scribble. 'What's her home address?'

The Faculty Administrator gave an address in Balfron.

'Married, then?' said Abernethy.

'Well, her father is David Bentley, well established solicitor in the city of Glasgow.'

'Thank you,' said Abernethy. 'Thank you very much indeed.' He replaced the receiver and dialled a two-figure internal number.

'Collator,' said a voice on the other end of the line.

'DC Abernethy here,' said Abernethy. 'Enquiring in respect of one Veronica Bentley, twenty years of age. Is she still listed as an m.p.?'

'One moment, please.'

Abernethy waited. In the background he heard the soft and rapid tapping of a computer keyboard.

'Yes, she is,' said the collator. 'Have there been developments?'

'Possibly,' said Abernethy. 'That's all I can say at present. But thanks anyway.' He replaced the phone and dialled another two-figure internal number.

'DI Donoghue,' said a crisp voice in Abernethy's ear.

'Abernethy, sir. The girl in question seems to be one Veronica Bentley, address in Balfron, daughter of David Bentley, solicitor.'

'Not only that, but one of the city's foremost solicitors. I know him, or rather know of him. If a felon engages the services of David Bentley, then the Fiscal's Office knows that it's in for a battle if they're going to secure a conviction. He does a lot of Legal Aid work for the humble and the lowly. He is on record as saying that it helps to keep him versatile.'

'I see, sir. Veronica Bentley was reported as missing on the twenty-first of January and is still on the m.p. list.'

'I see. Well, another bit of the jigsaw slots into place, or does it muddy the waters even more?'

'Sorry, sir?'

'Never mind. Write that information up, will you, and place it in the file on Eddie Wroe. The file's here on my desk.'

The soil in Lanarkshire is notoriously stony. Before the advent of fertilizers, the farmers of the county used to divide their land into parallel strips of three. The topsoil from the two outside strips was placed on the centre strip, thus providing sufficient soil with which to cultivate crops. Such strips of land were known as Long Riggs. At the site of the end of one such Long Rigg, long since disappeared, the Scottish Office built a Junior Remand Centre. On a Wednesday in early April, Detective-Inspector Donoghue and Detective-Sergeant Sussock drove out to Longriggend Remand Centre to interview Shane Dodemaide, remanded by the Glasgow Sheriff, having been charged with the murder of Eddie Wroe.

'It wisnae me,' said Dodemaide.

'Thought you might say that.' Donoghue relaxed in his chair. Beside him, Sussock shuffled uncomfortably. Shane Dodemaide sat shivering, huddled against the radiator that was built into the wall of the 'agent's room'. Beads of sweat ran down his forehead, he clutched his arms about his chest, the blue-striped, heavy gauge cotton shirt fitted him badly; it was baggy and outsize.

'Well, it wasn't.' Dodemaide ran the back of his hand under his nose. 'They say it's no worse than a dose of 'flu, but how would they know. They say it's in my head, but I didn't know my head was in my belly and in my arms and legs.'

'So who stabbed Eddie Wroe?' Donoghue said, quietly. 'Who stabbed him half a dozen times, if not your goodself, and how come your prints are on the knife that we found by the body?'

Shane Dodemaide shook his head as he clenched his teeth.

'Shane, you're not helping yourself. You've been in here for less than three days, enough to give you a taste of what's in store. Mind you, you've done a wee stretch before, but this time it's not the ninety days that you can do on your back, this time you're looking at a ten-year stretch. Institutionalization will set in after eight years, so when you come out you'll be a Salvation Army hostel case.' Donoghue paused. 'I suppose you're not too far from the bottom of the pecking order; you're not a big guy, you're not a tobacco baron, you're not big enough in the drug trade to have it smuggled in to you—am I right?'

Dodemaide nodded, a frightened man.

'So how does a ten-year stretch in the slammer sound?'

Dodemaide looked at Donoghue and then at the older, craggier-faced cop who sat behind the smartly dressed one and seemed to say nothing. Then he looked up at the thick, opaque glass set high in the wall and then he turned his head at the sound of the clanging gates echoing in the hall outside the agent's room.

'Doesn't sound so good, does it?' Donoghue said.

Dodemaide shook his head.

'If you don't help us, then we can't help you and we'll let you go the whole road. We'll let a jury decide whether you're guilty or not and we can build a very impressive case.'

'How can I help you?' Dodemaide pleaded in exasperation. 'I know nothing.'

'Tell us about your girlfriend.'

'I don't have a girl. Not right now anyway.'

'Well, in that case tell us about a girl called Veronica Bentley.'

'Oh, Veronica.'

'Yes, Veronica. Tall girl. Dark hair. Left the squat on Belmont Street a few weeks ago.'

'She moved in one dark night and moved out again one dark night. Stayed for a few weeks. Didn't go out at all in that time, stayed in, shot up, lived on cake and buns and tea. Me and Eddie, we kept her supplied with enough to keep her satisfied.'

'And I understand that she kept you satisfied in other ways.'

'That's just the way of it.'

'How did she know about the squat?'

'Eddie met her. I think it was Eddie who started her off, gave her some smack to try, pretty soon she was buying it from him.'

'I see.' Donoghue sighed. 'And that, too, I suppose is just the way of it?'

Dodemaide shrugged. 'So I think they met up a few times in a bar in Byres Road and eventually she moved in with him. She moved in with us really, but Eddie mainly.'

'Do you know how long Eddie and Veronica were seeing each other before she moved into the squat?'

'A few weeks; just before Christmas it was. I remember him telling me about this classy chick that he'd met and who was nipping him for smack. Then at the end of January or the beginning of February the self-same classy chick walks in off the street, wet, soaked, one plastic carrier bag with all her possessions inside. She took the top room but spent most of her time in Eddie's room.'

'So when did you and Eddie start sharing her?'

'When I had smack and he hadn't. First time was about two weeks after she moved in.'

'And when he had smack and you hadn't?'

'She went back to his room.'

'You and Eddie didn't come to blows over this?'

111

Dodemaide smiled. 'Well, there was always this under-standing that she was Eddie's girl, not mine. But it really wasn't important. It's not important how you get it or where or who you get it from, it's just important that you get it. I understand it, Eddie understood it, and Veronica under-stood it. Me and Eddie, we got money by screwing people's cars and turning their windows and knocking over old ladies and pinching their handbags.'

Donoghue looked at Dodemaide and saw a steely gleam in the young man's eyes. He saw a ruthlessness and an uncompromising viciousness and he momentarily didn't mind if this particular ned went down for a ten-year stretch.

'Knocking over old ladies,' Donoghue repeated.

'Look, I'm helping you to help me, like you said. I'm laying it on the line, I'm telling you how it is. See, the only rule is that there is no rule.'

'That's a contradiction.'

'Put it simply,' said Dodemaide, forcing a smile, getting cocky despite the cramps, 'we would do anything, anything at all for smack. I still would.'

'Anything else you can tell us about Veronica Bentley?'

'Law student drop-out. Her father is a big shot.'

'We know.'

'He was defending Eddie on a charge, theft by OLP, I think.'

Donoghue sat forward. 'Say that again.'

'Veronica's father was defending Eddie on a charge of theft by opening lockfast premises.'

'Well, well.' Donoghue sat back in his chair. 'Well, well, well.'

'Is that important?'

'Perhaps. Perhaps it's just an amazing coincidence, though I confess that I do find this big rambling city to be quite a small town at times. Did Veronica know that Eddie Wroe was being represented by her father?'

Dodemaide shook his head. 'No,' he said, then smiled an unpleasant smile, another unpleasant, thin-lipped smile. 'See, Eddie told me, told me not to tell Veronica. He told me that he kept pestering Bentley for appointments because

112

it gave him a kick. He'd sit in Bentley's office knowing that the man was sneering at him and all the while Eddie was thinking: See, you, you can smile all you like, but it's your daughter that's on my mattress and it's my smack that's in her veins. He got a real kick out of it.'

'Nice bloke, the late Eddie Wroe.'

'Sometimes he'd go to Bentley's office without an appointment and just wait in the waiting-room, just wanting to catch a glimpse of Bentley, refusing to be seen by one of Bentley's junior solicitors; he wanted to see Bentley and then go to the squat and give Veronica a freebie and Veronica would snatch it from him and shoot up. Like I said, it gave him a kick. He said I should use him too and I did. I got the same kick.'

'I dare say you would if you were twisted enough,' said Donoghue, 'and it sounds as though you are.'

'We had to hide all the letters that came from Bentley and Co. in case Veronica saw them. There wasn't much chance of her seeing them, she stayed upstairs all the time, just looking out of the window, shooting up, eating sticky buns that me and Eddie or Karen or Nick McQueen brought in.'

'Then one day Veronica left.'

'Left twice, in fact.'

'Oh?'

'Yes, she went away for a day, not an overnight, just a day. She came back, but it was a big thing that she went away at all. That was a big, big thing for her.'

'Did she say where she went?'

'No.' Shane Dodemaide shook his head. 'But I think that she saw her father.'

'What makes you say that?'

'Didn't make the connection at first, but later I worked out that it must be him; she just muttered something about being controlled by him.'

'Him? Could she mean Eddie Wroe?'

'I didn't think so. Still don't.' Dodemaide clutched his stomach. 'See, Eddie had no more control over her than I did and I had none. OK, she was nipping us for smack, but there was a hundred other guys in the city that she could nip just as easily.'

'Can you remember her words, exactly?'

'She said, "I can't escape. He controls me." She was speaking to herself and sort of shaking her head at the time, and then one day she wasn't there any more either.'

Donoghue and Sussock drove back to Glasgow, gazing out across the wild windswept hills of Lanarkshire. Donoghue said, 'What do you think, Ray?'

'I think it stinks, sir,' replied Sussock.

'I think it does, too. I think we will have to pay a call on Mr Bentley, respected solicitor of this fair town.'

Richard King glanced at his watch and drew breath between his teeth. He gently disentangled himself from Iain and inched gradually away from the tower of brightly coloured plastic bricks that they had spent the last five minutes building. He stood and Iain gave a wail of protest. King stooped and picked up his son and walked with him into the kitchen where Rosemary stood, slender and graceful in a pastel-coloured skirt. She was a committed Quaker, of Quaker parents, never wore trousers or loud colours and never spoke in harsh tones or a raised voice. She practised a high-minded aspect of Christianity which he, while fully respecting it, found impossible to embrace. He was a cop. Cops are cynical. Not only are they cynical but they are cynical before their time.

'Do you have time for a coffee or tea before you leave, Richard?'

King shook his head and handed Iain to Rosemary. ''Fraid not.' Standing up against the wall, behind and to the side of Rosemary, he noticed wood that he had bought the previous November, promising sincerely to put up shelves for her. The wood stood against the wall in exactly the place where he had laid it as he staggered in out of the rain, muttering something about a quick cup of coffee, and then he'd make an immediate start. She had not mentioned the shelves to him once and he knew that she never would, but she would, as many a Quaker would and as was her

Quakerly way, occasionally glance at them when he was in the kitchen and she knew that he was looking at her.

'I've got a few days' leave to take,' he said, reaching for his jacket. 'If all goes well, I'll put the shelves up for you then.'

'That would be nice, Richard.' She smiled a warm smile from lips that had never known lipstick and from a pleasantly balanced face that had never known make-up, above and beside which hung straight, shoulder-length hair which was washed only in herbal shampoo.

'Well, it's been long enough,' he said, but privately doubted that he'd get round to putting them up; Iain always proved too delightful a diversion to resist.

She kissed him and asked him to take care. She stood at the doorway until he had driven from her sight.

Abernethy was at his desk, tidying the surface, putting pens in drawers. He had evidently noticed that a clean desk makes a better impression than a good arrest rate. He nodded and smiled as King entered the room.

'Anything doing?' King unbuttoned his jacket.

Abernethy shook his head. 'Not a thing.'

'Don't like the calm before the storm.' King hung his jacket on the peg by the radiator.

'Still as wet as ever out there?' Abernethy glanced at the window.

'Well, as you see . . .'

'I was living in hope that this was highly localized.' Abernethy stood. 'Localized to about three streets in either direction, beyond which the sun shines down lovingly on old Scotia.'

'We may all live in hope, my son.' King reached for an early edition of the *Evening Times* which lay crumpled in his in-tray.

Abernethy drove home. He walked up a dark stair where rainwater dripped and plopped into a bucket, a stair which smelled of damp. At top right was a heavily stained door with 'Abernethy' embossed on a highly polished brass plate. He unlocked the door and let himself in and turned left into a dim bedroom.

'That you, son?' said a voice from the gloom.

'Yes, Dad. Did the nurse come?'

'Yes. What time is it?'

'Little after five-thirty.'

'In the evening?'

'Yes.'

'That you, son?'

'Yes, Dad.'

'You home, son?'

'Yes.'

'What time is it?'

'Five-thirty, just gone.'

'Are you staying in?'

'Yes, Dad.'

'What day is it?'

'Wednesday.'

'Time, please?'

'Five-thirty in the evening.'

'Thank you, son.'

Abernethy shut the door. He walked to the living-room still with the original fireplace range and a bed in the recess, the room in which he had grown up, the only son of elderly parents. 'A little gift late in life you were for us, son,' they had used to say, and his peers would say that they saw him in the park with his grandparents. He sank into the armchair by the fire and bent down to tug at his shoelaces. He pondered the report that he had written about the suicide that he had attended, the report that he had placed in Fabian Donoghue's in-tray, the report about the man who had taped wires to either hand and plugged himself not into the mains but into a timer switch. Then he had calmly sat and waited until 2.0 p.m. when the timing device had switched itself on.

It was clearly suicide. There was no evidence of foul play and the man was not restrained in any way. He could easily have torn off the wires at the last second, just one wire would have been enough to break the circuit, but he had gone through with it, one wire from the timing device taped to each hand and the timing device plugged into the mains,

116

just ticking on towards 2.0 p.m. Abernethy wondered what had gone through the man's mind during those last minutes, or was it hours, for how long had he sat waiting for the charge to jolt his body into lifelessness? He could have set the device to switch on up to twenty-four hours beforehand, or had he allowed himself just minutes to live? The man had been active and in good health, a keen hillwalker and summertime mountaineer. He lived life to the full and then, in his fortieth year, when fortunately still single and with no dependants, he was struck down with a wasting disease. He had nobody to live for and he did not want to experience the poor and degenerating quality of life that was ahead of him. The elaborate planning, the settling of debts, the recent will, the steps taken to ensure he was not discovered, the calm, reasoning, logical suicide note, the general lack of exhibitionism, meant that this was a suicide of the least suspicious kind. It was the man's life to take if he wished. He was of sound mind and he did what he wanted to do. Abernethy was pleased for him, in the kindest possible way, but none the less the man's last act in life had upset him. He was still inexperienced enough to be shocked by the actions of his fellow men.

Donoghue drove up to the house, a solid four-square, confident-looking building with tall windows and an impressive doorway, painted white, surrounded by green lawns and greener shrubs, dark blue mountains behind with just a trace of snow on the upper reaches, blue-grey sky above. There was a respite from the rain and he could see the distance clearly. He had dropped Ray Sussock in the city centre and had begun the drive home to Edinburgh when, on an impulse, he had driven northwards, out towards Balfron, to the home of David Bentley, solicitor; home address of Veronica Bentley, missing person.

Donoghue drove his Rover up to the front door and parked on he gravel beside a light blue Bentley. He got out of the Rover and shut the door noisily. People who live in houses of this ilk do not like to be come upon suddenly. The ringing of a doorbell is all very well in the schemes and the suburbs, but the owners of homes of this nature appreciate preliminary warning of the doorbell being rung. The sound of his tyres on the gravel and the slamming of the car door had had the desired effect. The front door of the house swung silently open as he approached it.

A woman stood in the doorway. She was slightly built but plump about the face and had a page-boy haircut which might have suited her if she had been twenty years younger. She wore flat, sensible shoes. She reminded Donoghue of Richard King's wife, but whereas he had found Rosemary King to be a young woman of steel behind her humility, this woman had a lost and frightened look about her.

'Yes?' she said meekly, apologetically, not at all the lady-of-the-house greeting a stranger on the threshold of her property. 'May I help you?'

'Police,' said Donoghue.

'Oh,' she whimpered.

'About Veronica.'

'Oh, she's better, she's much better. She's been keeping solids down.'

'What do you mean?' Donoghue allowed an edge to creep into his voice. 'Do you know where she is?'

'Well, yes,' said the woman in a timid voice. 'She's out.'

'Out?'

'Upstairs. She's upstairs in her room. Sorry, I'm a bit confused. She went out earlier in the day, but now she's back. Out for a little walk.'

'Why weren't we informed?'

'Informed of what?'

'That she's here. She is still listed as a missing person. You're Mrs Bentley, her mother?'

'Yes.' The woman wrung her hands. 'I didn't know that Veronica was still listed as missing. Mr Bentley sees to things like that. He makes all the difficult decisions.'

'I think I'd like to have a word with him.'

The woman looked frightened and glanced at her husband's car.

'There's not a great deal of point in telling me that he's out.' Donoghue spoke quietly.

118

'If you'd step this way, please.' She turned. Donoghue swept his homburg off as he stepped over the threshold. The hallway was expansive, with Corinthian columns at either side of a wide stairway. It smelled heavily of wood polish and a whiff of disinfectant. Above all, it was quiet. Oppressively so. Even a ticking clock would have been welcome.

The woman opened a door on the left of the hallway. It was a heavy wide door with a knob at waist height as was the fashion in Victorian Britain and was much more sensible, in Donoghue's view, than the handles set at shoulder height so often found in the modern 'new build' homes, homes like his own bungalow.

'If you'd like to wait in here, sir,' she said, pushing the door open and standing to one side, inviting him to enter the room with a flowing movement of her forearm.

The room was a library. The walls were lined with books; a fourth wall was taken up by two tall windows with a bronze-painted radiator underneath. Through the window Donoghue could see his car and Bentley's Bentley, the gravel drive, the lawn, the shrubs and the gateway at the bottom of the drive. In the centre of the room was a huge, lavishly polished table, so huge that Donoghue fancied that one of the tall window-frames would have had to be removed from the stonework and the table manhandled sideways into the room. It was far too large to have been carried in through the doorway. On the table stood a vase of flowers and an ornamental wooden case about the size of a small suitcase. Upholstered chairs stood around the table, one at either end, four down each side.

Donoghue was in the room for a full five minutes before the homeowner deigned to appear. The door opened with a gentle click. Donoghue turned and stared at one of the tallest men, certainly the largest man, he had ever seen. Donoghue as a police officer was used to being taller than average and was used to looking into the eyes of his colleagues, but when he was confronted by David Bentley, he received a sudden and vivid insight into the world of small men.

Donoghue put Bentley's height at six and a half feet

119

minimum, but not only was the man tall but he was of impressive bulk, not bloated or run to fat, but muscular, in good shape, perfectly proportioned, broad-shouldered, broad-chested, with legs the same length as his spine. He wore a pale blue suit and tie, the same blue as his car, and a white silk shirt. He had a flat face, with a small nose.

He had piercing blue eyes which held Donoghue's gaze.

The two men stood staring at each other, Donoghue feeling small and vulnerable as he stood in the centre of the room, Bentley standing half in the room, holding the door open, saying nothing, not showing any facial expression, save a forced mood of seriousness.

Donoghue thought: I'll hold his stare, he'll have to speak first.

But Bentley just stood and stared, not moving, not even blinking.

Seconds dragged.

Donoghue began to feel a gnawing fear of the man which ate at the very fabric of the mantle of authority that he wore as a police officer.

Still the man spoke not a word, nor did he move so much as a muscle.

Before he knew what he was doing, Donoghue said, 'I'm Detective-Inspector Donoghue, P Division, at Charing Cross.' Then as if rewarding Donoghue, Bentley smiled, stepped fully into the room with extended hand.

Donoghue hesitated. Bentley held his hand out and continued to smile.

Again, seconds dragged by.

Eventually Donoghue extended his hand and it was grasped by the clammy paw of David Bentley of the cold eye.

'How can I help you, Inspector?' Bentley smiled.

'I've called about your daughter, sir. She's still listed as a missing person, but your wife has just informed me that Veronica is upstairs.'

'I know, I know, I have spoken to her, my dear Inspector. How can I apologize enough? What can I say? We did wonder why the police had not called to verify that she was safe, that she had returned.'

'So what happened? You seem to have withheld information from the police.'

'It's the old story, Inspector. I thought that my wife had done it and vice versa.'

It didn't ring true, but Donoghue let it ride.

'I don't think I've met you before, Inspector. I know many policemen, but I don't think I've had the pleasure?' A smile. A gleam in the eye.

'No. I don't think we have met.'

'A drink?'

'I can't. But thanks anyway.'

'Of course you can't. I was forgetting. Are you a family man, too?'

'Yes, I am. Why do you ask?'

'No reason, just curious. It was fortunate that my wife showed you in here. I was coming in here to clean my guns.'

'Your guns?'

'The box here.' Bentley moved silently and effortlessly across the carpet and reached for the box which stood on the table. He opened the catches and lifted the lid. Inside the velvet-lined box were two silver, pearl-handled revolvers and a row of bullets.

'I hope you're impressed?' he said. 'They are, of course, registered, I have a licence and I keep the box in a safe.'

'Of course,' said Donoghue, unimpressed. He did not like guns. He did not like scratched and battered First World War Walthers in the hands of money-lenders, or pearl-handled revolvers in the hands of solicitors. Guns were guns and he didn't like them.

Bentley picked one of the revolvers from the case and fondled it lovingly. He held it in one hand and ran the fingers of the other along the barrel. He handed it to Donoghue, butt first.

'No.' Donoghue shook his head. 'I don't like guns.'

'They are my one pleasure,' said Bentley. 'I find being the head of a family and the head of a firm of solicitors a lonely business. No colleagues in either role. No—what's the term?—lateral support, that's it, no lateral support.'

'Indeed?'

'You and I must be about the same age, same generation anyway.' Bentley held the gun and drew back the hammer. 'I grew up alone. Did you have any brothers or sisters?' He released the hammer gently.

'Yes, I did.'

'You know, I would have liked a brother. Never had one.' He replaced the gun back inside the presentation case. Donoghue felt uneasy in Bentley's presence. Perhaps it was just years of police work, perhaps it was human instinct, but he felt that he was being drawn into a wholly inappropriate collusion with a very dangerous person.

'I'd like to see your daughter, sir.'

'Of course.'

'We have to see her in order to close the missing person file.'

'Of course, I'll bring . . . I'll have her come down.'

'I'll go to her room if she's ill. Mrs Bentley indicated as much.'

'She's ill, but quite able to walk.' Bentley smiled at Donoghue.

'Ill?'

'Just ill. But recovering.' Bentley turned. 'If you'd wait here.'

'I know that she is a heroin addict.'

Bentley halted and Donoghue thought that he collected himself just in time to avoid throwing a glare at him.

'Then there isn't any point in trying to hide it from you?' Again Bentley smiled a warm, colluding smile.

'No, sir, there isn't.'

Bentley left the room. Donoghue heard him call 'Miriam, have Veronica come down to the library . . . yes, now!' Bentley returned. 'Took me a long time to collect the books,' he said. 'There's seven thousand of them in this room. Many of them first editions.'

'Really,' said Donoghue, still feeling unsure, still feeling himself to be on unfamiliar territory.

'Collect anything yourself?' A beaming smile.

122

Donoghue shook his head. 'Can't say that I do.'

'Oh.'

There was a footfall in the hallway, two pairs of feet, softly shuffling. A knock at the door of the room.

'Come in,' said Bentley.

The door swung open. A figure glided into the room and Donoghue caught his breath. Once, he thought, once she had probably been quite beautiful. Now she was drawn, deathly white, as white as the gown she wore. Her cheeks were hollow and sunken, her hair was dull and lifeless, her eyes had sunk in their sockets.

'My daughter Veronica,' said Bentley. 'Whom I love deeply.'

Veronica shot a glance at her father. His hand flinched.

Veronica pulled her head back and stepped to one side.

And Donoghue, watching, observing, felt a sudden chill run through him: there was something about the man's manner, the apparently jovial attitude that was betrayed by a coldness of his eyes and the sudden curtness, and the equally sudden flash of temper . . . Donoghue had read and heard of such men. He would seek learned advice.

CHAPTER 8

Thursday, 09.45–18.00 hours

'How long have I got?' The man smiled. He had a round jovial face, but eyes which spoke of serious intent. 'You know the popular reply to your question is to say, "Well, I can't describe an elephant, but I know one when I see one."'

'I see. Do you mind if I smoke, sir?' Donoghue took his pipe from his pocket.

'Not at all.' Dr Cass grinned. 'In fact, I'll join you. Do you want to try my tobacco?' He proffered a tin.

'A bit strong for my taste, sir.' Donoghue took his pipe

from his pocket. 'Try mine. It's a mix I have made up specially.'

'Sounds interesting.' Cass scraped his pipe bowl into the ashtray and filled his pipe with Donoghue's mixture. Donoghue glanced around Cass's office. The desk was healthily untidy, strewn with papers, the walls were lined with books, there were plants on the window-sill. The window itself looked out across an open grassed area which was surrounded by university buildings. The rain fell vertically.

That morning, after a troubled and restless sleep, he had phoned the university, requesting an audience with a psychiatrist. If none had been available, he would have telephoned the psychiatric hospitals until he located a psychiatrist who was prepared to give up his or her time for him. Come what may, he had to consult a psychiatrist and do so with a degree of urgency. He struck lucky with the first phone call. Dr Cass could offer him an hour between 10.0 and 11.0 a.m. Donoghue arrived at Cass's office at 09.45, shook the rain from his coat and handed it to the secretary who smilingly hung it on the peg on the door. The secretary showed Donoghue into Dr Cass's study. Cass stood and extended his hand. He had a firm, genuine grip and Donoghue liked the man instantly.

'How can I help you, Inspector?' Cass indicated a chair which stood in front of his desk.

'Thank you, sir.' Donoghue relaxed into the chair. 'Well, I'd like some information, sir. I'd like to know what exactly is meant by the term "psychopath"?'

Cass smiled and made mention of the elephant. He returned Donoghue's tobacco pouch and Donoghue commenced the filling of his own pipe. As one pipe-smoker would to another, Cass waited until Donoghue had completed the ritual of filling his pipe and then of lighting it until the tobacco smouldered to his satisfaction and until Donoghue had relaxed back in the easy chair, savouring the smoke. Then he spoke.

'Well,' he said, 'the first thing to understand is that the term "psychopath" is a lay term and, despite the fact

124

that all the papers have been written by psychiatrists, psychopathy is not a recognized or treatable psychiatric condition. A psychopath's personality does not break down as would be the case if he were mentally ill. Someone may be dubbed a psychopathic killer by the media when at large, and then, when apprehended and imprisoned, his personality collapses, indicating that that person has been mentally ill all along. A true dyed-in-the-wool psychopath will retain his or her personality while in gaol, throughout a long-term sentence, even life, and will continue to convince himself and all who will listen of his innocence. Or, if he concedes guilt at all, he will concede partial guilt, saying for instance, "Well, I did kill two people, but not the six or seven or whatever that they blamed me for."'

'I see.' Donoghue nodded, already intrigued.

'Or again, if he concedes guilt, he will attempt to blame others. This is a bit difficult to describe, but a psychopath will offer not just a limp excuse for his crime but a circuitous argument which defies logic or reason. He may, for instance, say something like, "Well, yes, I did embezzle all that money over a period of years, but Personnel had it in for me and had blocked my promotion. So I was the victim all along."'

Donoghue caught his breath.

'Sounds familiar, Inspector?'

'Painfully so.' Donoghue nodded. 'Usually just with petty criminals, though. I have tended to associate the label psychopath with dangerous criminals.'

Cass cradled his pipe in his hands and Donoghue felt relaxed and thought that students must enjoy tutorials with this man.

'You've very cleverly struck two nails on the head with a single sentence,' Cass said, smiling.

'I have?'

'Yes. Point one is that psychopathic behaviour is more anti-social or asocial than it is bordering on insanity. As I indicated earlier, psychopaths are perfectly sane. It is for that reason that the American term "sociopath" is gaining currency this side of the herring pond. It's a term which more accurately describes the condition than does "psychopath", which carries with it a wholly erroneous suggestion of insanity.'

The telephone on Cass's desk rang. He ignored it. It rang twice and was then silent.

'Donna, my secretary, has caught it,' he explained. 'You see, the first point is that, for the most part, psychopaths' behaviour is of a petty criminal type or just plain anti-social. And the second point that you hit upon is that we have been able to identify three groups or types of psychopaths or sociopaths. The inadequate, the creative and the dangerous.'

'Really?'

'Yes. So lelt us take them in that order. The inadequate, well, he's the chap that you blokes come across time and time again. The neds, as you might say. They are incompetent, they get involved in petty crime, always in and out of gaol, and they will always blame someone else for their misfortune. The second group is the creative. Now these are successful people in terms of achievement, but their personal behaviour is destructive; people in this group would include artists, composers, captains of industry.'

'Successful solicitors?'

'Anything. Anything at all. But despite their success, they are unable to deal with relationships and can damage without remorse or guilt. The third group is the one that gets all the media attention and that is the so-called "aggressive" group. These are the mass murderers, the serial killers. This group shows a lack of emotional response, they enjoy killing and feel no remorse. They can be heroes in wartime.'

Donoghue nodded reverently.

'All psychopaths are intelligent and articulate. Even the so-called "inadequate" group. Any crime they commit is often bizarre, well-planned and intricate, and here you have the hallmarks of a psychopathic crime. You see, Inspector, someone who is seriously mentally ill will kill at random and will leave the body where it fell, where it can be found, and will run off into the night. A psychopath, on the other hand, now he's the boy who will choose his victim, plan the

126

murder, often prolonging it with ritual, or may convince the victim that he is not going to be murdered and will eventually be released from captivity, and who will dispose of the body in such a way that it will not easily be found, burying it, for example. Alternatively, he may leave the body where it is easily found, but do so in order to implicate an innocent party.'

'Funny that you should say that,' said Donoghue.

'Really?'

'Yes. All I can say at the moment is that it strikes relevant notes.'

'I see. Well, I'm pleased that I am being of assistance. The numbers of aggressive psychopaths are fortunately low. There are probably about forty or fifty in British prisons at the moment, which means that there are about four times that number in the community.'

'That's frightening.'

'Well, it's not as chilling as it sounds because many of those aggressive psychopaths will be latent, or will be controlled within their particular social framework. Again, we come to the difference between a mentally ill person, the "mad" rather than the "bad", the psychopath. The "mad" person will not be contained, the "bad" will.'

'Because the "mad" person is ill?'

'Precisely,' said Cass. 'You see, psychopaths need not only their psychopathic personalities but also a precise set of circumstances which will enable them to commit a crime and get away with it in order for them to pass from latency to activity.'

'So,' said Donoghue, 'the potential is constant, always there, and when it comes together with opportunity, which is not constant, then the potential of the aggressive psychopath is released?'

'Very well put, Inspector.'

'So it's possible for an aggressive psychopath to live out his life without committing a crime?'

'Yes. If the opportunity to commit a serious crime never presents itself, then he won't commit that crime. A "mad" person, on the other hand, is capable of running amok with a knife in a crowded street in broad daylight. I really don't know what else I can tell you, Inspector. People known as psychopaths tend to "act" rather than "live", they will act out the role of a family man, go through the motions, but won't "live" it. Another favoured phrase to describe a psychopath is "He knows the words but not the music."'

'He appears normal?'

'Yes. In fact, of all the key characteristics of the psychopath, that is the cornerstone. You see, the whole purpose of criminal psychopathy is getting away with the crime. It is therefore vital to appear normal, the last thing an aggressive psychopath wants to do is to draw attention to himself. Having said that, his crimes are so convoluted and complicated that that is what he does do, draws attention to himself. The more you analyse his crime, the more it becomes obvious who it was that committed the crime, no matter how hard he or she tries to throw you off the scent. This is why the inadequate groups go in and out of gaol as often as they do.'

'I see. This is fascinating, sir.'

'It's all off the top of my head. I can recommend some good reading. Other characteristics might be, well, absence of delusions or fantasy or other signs of irrational thought, a lack of nervousness, great calm and self-control, a lack of truthfulness, a lack of sincerity, lack of guilt feelings or feelings of remorse or shame, a great egocentricity, a lack of wealth of the major affective reactions.'

'Inability to love, for example?'

'Inability to hate as well; a lack of anger, a lack of enthusiasm, lack of fear, generally a lack of the major emotions which go to make up a normal human being.'

'Extreme detachment?'

'Yes. Psychopaths are generally unresponsive in personal relationships; their sex life is trivial, impersonal and poorly integrated. One other major characteristic, and probably the most frightening, is an apparent ability to influence and control other people. It is as if a psychopath can cast a spell over people in his immediate circle, it may only be one person or two, but these people will fall under his control.

128

Beware of an over-friendly approach, a laying on of hands even, resting a hand on your leg, shaking your hand with an over-long eye contact, or reaching out on an emotional plane, inviting you to be a role model he or she never had— "You know, I never had a father," for instance. Beware of that, it's the beginning of the snare that will eventually trap you.'

'Like a spider's web.' Donoghue tapped his pipe in the ashtray, sensing that it was time to go, to thank and conclude.

'That's an analogy worth remembering.' Cass stood, taking Donoghue's eye. 'If only because in terms of proportion to their actual size, spiders have the largest jaws of any living creature. Psychopaths rarely commit suicide, tend to be Caucasian, tend to have relocated from their roots, tend to be only children. That's just off the top of my head.'

'Thank you, sir,' said Donoghue.

It was Thursday, 11.05 hrs.

Donoghue drove out to Balfron, the house of Bentley, as he would later write in officialese. Ray Sussock sat beside him and said nothing, speaking only when spoken to and then giving little in exchange. Donoghue sensed that the older man was in a huff; better to just let him brood, he reasoned.

Donoghue drove the Rover up to the imposing Bentley residence. The rain had eased off and then stopped, a temporary respite; the sun shone brightly through a gap in the cloud cover and, as the police officers got out of the Rover, their nostrils were assailed by the scent of plants: everything about them smelled fresh and new and cleansed. Donoghue and Sussock climbed up the steps of the house and Donoghue reached forward and pressed the doorbell. It rang, jangling and hollowly echoing in the vast hallway. Sussock turned and surveyed the panorama of hills and white-painted cottages and trees; his eye fell lovingly and longingly on one cottage in particular, white like the others, nestling in a fold in the hills, isolated at the top of a long winding drive.

'Not bad,' he said in his first unsolicited statement of the afternoon, 'not bad at all.'

Donoghue was keen to respond, keen to jerk Sussock out of his mood. 'As they say, nice work if you can get it!'

The door opened. Mrs Bentley stood in the doorway, a retiring, whimpering woman with short black hair and flower-patterned frock. She held her hands tightly together.

'Yes, gentlemen?' she said in a thin, frightened voice. 'Mr Bentley's not at home.'

'That's all right. We'd like to talk to Veronica,' Donoghue said.

Miriam Bentley stepped aside and the two cops entered the clean-smelling hall, sweeping off their hats as they crossed the threshold.

'If you'd like to wait in the library, please. I'll bring her down.'

'She's still unwell?'

A look of guilt, or embarrassment perhaps, thought Donoghue, flashed across Miriam Bentley's eyes. 'It's nothing. A touch of cold and influenza.'

'Influenza?' Donoghue echoed. 'We're quite prepared to go upstairs.'

'No.'

'We'll go upstairs,' said Sussock.

'Well, if you insist, gentlemen.'

Donoghue raised his eyebrows. 'We insist.'

'Mr Bentley won't like it. He won't approve.'

'Just refer him to us,' said Sussock.

Miriam Bentley sighed and turned and ascended the wide staircase. Sussock and Donoghue followed. The staircase turned half way up and a large stained glass window looked down on the turn of the stair. On the upstairs landing Miriam Bentley turned to her right and walked along a carpeted corridor. She stopped at a door and took a key from her pocket.

Donoghue and Sussock glanced at each other.

'You keep her locked in the room?' said Sussock.

Miriam Bentley turned the key. 'My husband insists on it,' she said. 'I don't like it but he insists on it.'

130

'And you do as he says?'

Miriam Bentley nodded, as if to say, 'Yes, I know it's wrong, but I do it. I don't know why I do it, but I do.' She flung the door wide. 'Some people to see you, dear.'

Veronica Bentley lay in bed under sheets and blankets. She was pale, drawn, hungry-looking, her long black hair lay on the pillow. She levered herself up and as her strength seemed to seep from her, she sank back on to the pillow.

Donoghue glanced around the room. The bed was an old hospital bed, he thought, metal frame painted a sickly creamy yellow colour and flaking here and there. The floorboards were bare, the windows were curtainless. There was not the smallest item of furnishing in the room, save the bed. And that was it, an utterly naked room, a metal bed, two sheets, two blankets, a pillow, a girl and pyjamas for the girl. Sussock crossed to the window and tried to open it.

'It's nailed shut,' said the girl. 'It gets a bit stuffy in here, but it's better than the shed in the garden.'

'The shed?'

'I started out in the shed.'

'Mr Bentley allowed Veronica back into the house once the worst was over,' said Miriam Bentley.

'The worst?'

'I'm a smack-head,' said Veronica Bentley.

'I know,' said Donoghue.

'Mr Bentley is doing that which is best.'

'So he says,' Veronica Bentley said sourly.

'What is he doing for the best?' asked Donoghue.

'Well, my husband says it's just like a dose of 'flu, any discomfort is all in her head.'

'That's what he said to me, so I said that I ache all over—my joints especially. The funny thing is, the only place I don't hurt is my head.'

'Veronica . . .' Miriam Bentley pleaded.

'Look, Mother, he's destroyed you, he's not destroying me. I've got a life of my own and most of it is still in front of me. See, him, he threw the baby out with the bathwater

131

years ago.' She turned to Donoghue. 'Can you take me out of here, please?'

'Veronica!'

'Can you take me away? I'm twenty years old. I can leave if I want. I'm a prisoner here.'

'Veronica, your father says it's for your own good.'

'Yes,' said Donoghue calmly. 'Yes, of course we'll take you out of here. Have you got any clothes or have they been nailed down too?'

'I don't know. Where are they, Mother? Perhaps he's destroyed them as a second line of defence to prevent my escape.'

'I can't let you have them.' Miriam Bentley shook nervously.

'I would, if I were you,' said Donoghue.

'Otherwise you are aiding and abetting unlawful imprisonment,' said Sussock.

'She's our daughter.'

'She's an adult.'

'I'm going, Mother.' Veronica Bentley propped herself up in the bed. 'I'd like to see a doctor.'

'I think you need one,' said Donoghue. He turned to the shaking woman. 'Can you get her some clothes, or take her to where her clothing is?'

'You'd better come too, Mother. You know he's only going to put your blood on the wall again, just as soon as he finds out that I'm gone.'

Miriam Bentley hesitated.

Donoghue said, 'It's up to you, Mrs Bentley. If you suffer mental violence, you can be offered alternative accommodation.'

'I don't know what to do for the best.'

'I want you to come with me, Mother.' Veronica Bentley levered herself out of bed. Donoghue saw that she had the potential to be very, very attractive, but at present she was thin and anæmic. 'We can make a fresh start.'

'In a council housing scheme?'

'It would be better than this prison.'

'Maybe I will. I don't know. I've been here most of my

132

life. I mean, how can I walk out on thirty years of marriage?'

'Easily.' Veronica Bentley stood unsteadily. 'Besides, I don't call what I've seen any sort of marriage. It's a wonder you've any teeth left.'

'I don't have much time.' Miriam Bentley glanced at her watch. 'He could come home any time now.'

'He can come home any time he likes,' said Donoghue. 'I know it's his house, but we are in control here.'

'No, he can't,' said Veronica. 'He has control over us, over her especially. You know what he's like, Mother. Face up to reality, will you?'

'I can't . . . I can't . . .'

'Will you come with me, or stay?'

'You're really going?'

'I have to. I want to live. I don't want this—this—this living death that you're living.'

'But thirty years of marriage, thirty years . . . it's half a life.'

'It's a half-life. There is a difference.'

'We'll wait downstairs,' said Donoghue.

'What did you want to see me about anyway?' Veronica Bentley forced a smile. 'Inspector Donoghue, isn't it?'

'We wanted a chat about Eddie Wroe and Shane Dodemaide.'

'Oh, them. Look, I was heavily into the poison then. I'm trying to put it all behind me. I'm not so pleased with myself, but when you're down where I was, all you care about is your next fix, all you want to do is puncture yourself and fill yourself up with poison.' She pulled up her pyjama sleeve and revealed a blotched, bruised skin with a series of small dots in the bruising. 'See my track marks,' she said. 'The bruising will fade, but the track marks will remain. Just in case I forget, they'll be there to remind me. So what's happened to Shane and Eddie? They're just sad cases, really. They're really victims. Have you pulled them for theft or something?'

'Not exactly,' said Donoghue.

'Oh?'

'Shane Dodemaide's in gaol.'

'Shane in the slammer?'

'Afraid so.'

'Why?'

'Murder.'

'Oh no! Not Shane. Really, Inspector, he's done a few daft things in his time, but he wouldn't murder anybody. He hasn't got the bottle for that. He wouldn't murder anyone.'

'Well, frankly, between you and me and Sergeant Sussock here, I'm inclined to believe you. But the circumstantial evidence is so strong that we can't ignore it.'

'His fingerprints were found on what we believe may have been the murder weapon,' said Sussock by means of explanation.

'Well, that's damning enough,' Veronica Bentley conceded. 'So what about Eddie? Is he implicated as well?'

'No,' said Donoghue. 'He is the deceased in question.'

Sussock drove to Longriggend. He had journeyed back to P Division with Donoghue. In the rear of the Rover had sat a pale-faced Veronica Bentley and a lost-looking Miriam Bentley; both seemed to be in a state of shock, especially, thought Sussock, Miriam Bentley, who seemed to be a lady confronting a wasted past and an uncertain future. At Longriggend he was shown into the agent's room, the same agent's room where earlier he and Donoghue had interviewed Shane Dodemaide. Sussock sat on one of the chairs and rested his forearms on the table. In his mind he went over the questions that Donoghue had asked him to put— 'Don't feed him the answers, Ray, you know the form. I'll leave it to you.'

He waited a full ten minutes before Shane Dodemaide was shown into the room. When he entered, he looked sheepish and embarrassed. He was bruised about the face and had a long cut across his forehead. He grinned a forced grin and revealed a top gum with newly missing teeth.

'Finding your feet, Shane?' asked Sussock as the youth sat opposite him.

'I can't stand it in here, Mr Sussock.' Shane Dodemaide's

134

grin faded and gave way to a desperate pleading and expression of despair. 'I never killed nobody.'

'That's why I'm here.'

'You're here to help me? Last night they gave me a doing.' He waved a hand over his face. 'I've got more bruises under my shirt. I wouldn't put the slop bucket over my head and bunny-hop up and down the cell.'

'Aye, there's some hard wee neds in here. So if you want me to help you, you'll have to help us.'

'What do you want me to do, Mr Sussock?'

'Reach back into you memory. I know that your short-term memory is bad, the heroin does that to you, but I want you to think.'

Shane Dodemaide nodded.

'Two questions. First, the sequence of events from the time that Veronica came to the squat to the time we lifted you. I mean comings and goings, not when, but the sequence. Second, anything that happened to you in that time concerning Veronica's father. Take your time.'

'Well, I've got plenty of that.'

Sussock opened his notebook and took out his ballpoint pen.

'It's not so easy to remember, Mr Sussock. I don't remember too well.'

'Try,' Sussock spoke sharply. 'It's up to you. You can get out of here within hours if we drop the charges, or you can go back to your cell doing bunny-hops between the bunks with the slop bucket on your head. It's up to you. If you think that you're tough enough to do a ten-year stretch in the slammer, then just don't try to remember. But if you want out and back home . . .'

'Home!' Shane Dodemaide sighed.

'Or wherever, but out of here at any rate.'

'I want out.'

'Then help me to help you. How about those questions?'

'What were they again?'

'Sequence of comings and goings at the squat and anything that happened between you and Mr Bentley.'

135

'Oh yes. In January, it was cold and dark and wet and she came in shivering and bedraggled.'

'When did you realize that Eddie Wroe's solicitor was Veronica's father?'

'Eddie told me in mid-February. He was sort of amused by it. Kept making appointments to see Mr Bentley. Things went on like that for a few weeks as Eddie's case was coming up, theft by OLP, I think.'

'What did he turn over? A lock-up?'

'Something like that. Eddie was into stealing videos, very easy to unload. Two videos would buy a day's smack. He worked really hard, did Eddie. Made a lot of money. He'd get lifted, get lifted again, but just kept at it. He had to survive.'

'You did the same sort of thing?'

'Yes. He showed me the ropes, then we operated separately. We could keep each other supplied better. See, that way only one of us got lifted at any one time.'

'So Eddie was visiting Mr Bentley regularly. He went to see him at his office? Which is where?'

'In the town in Bath Street. One day I got lifted for possession, a few grains. I got bailed and Eddie said I should go and see Mr Bentley. He said that Bentley was a huge guy in a silk shirt getting fat on Legal Aid money and not really giving a damn about anybody, but you can sit there and think how we are passing his daughter backwards and forwards between us. That's what Eddie said.'

'Pleasant couple of guys, weren't you?'

Shane Dodemaide shrugged. 'I had a deprived childhood.'

'So did I, but I grew up to sit on this side of the table. I was one of six kids in a single end in the Gorbals and I mean the Gorbals. Anyway, so at one point you were both visiting Mr Bentley?'

'Yes.'

'So when did Veronica disappear?'

'Towards the middle of March. About two weeks ago.'

'I understand she went out for the day on one occasion?'

'Yes, a few days before she left for good she went out and stayed out all day.'

'Did she say where she had been?'

A shake of the head.

'And a few days later she disappeared?'

A nod of the head.

'So what happened between the time she went out for the day and came back and the time she went out for good?'

'Not a lot. We sat in and watched the rain. Karen went down the town in the evening and earned money that way. Me and Eddie did a bit of ducking and diving, a bit of bobbing and weaving, you know, just to keep the dosh rolling in and just keeping one step ahead of the polis, you guys, sat in a bit more, shot up three, four times a day, traded in old needles for clean works at the needle exchange.'

'That all?'

A shrug of the shoulders.

'Come on, think! Sit up and think.'

Shane Dodemaide shifted in his chair. 'I went to see Mr Bentley.'

'You made an appointment to see him so you could sneer at him?'

'No. He called me in.'

Sussock looked up. 'He called you in?'

'Yes. About two days after Veronica disappeared for the day, he called me in. I got a letter asking me to attend at his office the next afternoon.'

'What did he want to see you about?'

'Nothing, so far as I could tell. Just went over the same ground.'

'All right. What else happened?'

'Well, two days went by. Sat watching the rain and shooting up. Eddie said he was going to see Bentley.'

'Did Mr Bentley invite him for an appointment?'

'No. Eddie just fancied going to see him. Just a glimpse of him was all he wanted before he went back to the squat to roll his daughter. Well, that was last Friday. Eddie came back and said that he was to see Bentley again the next morning. Bentley wanted to see him.'

'He works on Saturdays?'

'Apparently. In the mornings anyway. He, Eddie, he went out at about ten a.m. that morning.'

'And that was the last you saw of him?'

'That was the last I saw of him.'

'His body was found less than twenty-four hours later. So what happened to him in the interim?'

'It's your job to find that out.'

'Not really that frightened of the slopman, are you?'

'What do you mean?'

'Well, I would have thought that a few days in here might have taught you something, but you've got a serious attitude problem, Shane. If you get off with this it'll only be a matter of months before you're back inside on another charge. Just think about that tonight after you've finished bunny-hopping between the bunks.'

'You're not taking me out now?'

'No. Maybe not for a few days.'

Colour drained from Dodemaide's face.

'I can't go back to the cell.'

'You're going back. You're still the prime suspect.'

'I didn't kill him. He was my pal.'

'So help us a bit more. Let's go back to your interview with Mr Bentley, the one you had shortly after Veronica went out for the day; the one he asked you in for at short notice, the one where he didn't seem to want much from you?'

'Just to go over my statements. Seeing as I was pleading guilty on all counts, I didn't see what there was to be anxious about.'

'How long were you in there with him?'

'Twenty minutes.'

'Anything happen while you were in there?'

'No. I sat in front of his desk, answered the same questions that I'd answered before. I thought he was just asking me in to fill up his time for his Legal Aid money.'

'Is that all?'

'Yes. Yes.'

'Anything else you did?' Sussock didn't know how to

proceed. He was mindful of Donoghue's advice, not to feed the youth the answer that was required.

Dodemaide looked at Sussock.

Sussock looked at Dodemaide. How to proceed?

'Anything happen that hadn't happened in the previous interviews?'

'No,' he said thoughtfully. 'No, it was just like the others.

Sussock paused. He didn't want to feed the answer, but he couldn't proceed without a suggestion of it. 'Did you touch anything?'

'A knife,' said Shane Dodemaide slowly, as if the significance was dawning on him as he spoke. 'He had an envelope on his desk. He wanted to cut it open. He asked me to pass a knife to him. There was a knife on the shelf behind me.'

'So you did?'

'Aye.'

'How did you hold the knife—by the blade?'

'No, by the handle, sort of backwards. I was all along taught by my old mother to hold a knife like that; see, her, if she ever taught us anything worth knowing, it was how to hold a knife if you're walking with it. My old man, he died in the house when he fell on a knife he was carrying. He was carrying it in front of him and pointed up the way. He fell on it as he tripped and it pierced his heart. So my mother said. So she said we had to hold the knife sort of behind and beside us. Also said that when we handed a knife to someone, it had to be handle first. So for two reasons when I took the knife off the shelf, I held it sort of backwards so I could walk across his office floor with it, safe like, and so I could hand it to him, handle first.'

'Did he take it from you?'

'No.' Shane Dodemaide shook his head. 'No, he didn't. He told me to put it on his desk, said he'd use it later. So I did. Then he said I could go; said he'd be in touch.'

'What sort of knife was it?'

'Wooden handle, short thin blade. Just a regular kitchen knife.'

*

139

They glanced at Tuesday Noon once and then forgot him. An old wino, sitting in a world of his own, one big glass and one little glass in front of him, pathetically almost empty of liquid. Tuesday Noon stared ahead of him at the darkly stained wood of the gantry and the frosted glass behind it. He didn't normally use this bar and had half, more than half, expected to be refused service; it often happened. The bar was empty when he entered and the young woman behind the bar eyed him with a pitying eye and allowed the old derelict to buy a beer and a whisky. He took the drinks to a table in the corner by the door. Not a lot was happening here, he thought; perhaps he'd spin out the drinks for half an hour and then move on to the next bar. There were plenty of bars in Woodlands, plenty of opportunity to catch sight or sound of something. Then they came in, a boy and girl, old enough to buy alcohol but only just, no money, denim, torn training shoes, dripping wet from the rain. They bought a drink and sat near him; they glanced at him once. Tuesday Noon looked straight ahead of him but strained his ears. He struck gold immediately.

'Easier,' said the girl. 'It's easier than the street.'

'Less dangerous.'

'Less money, though.'

'You never know. Some of these old birds carry their life savings around with them.'

'You didn't hit them so hard, no?'

'Just a tap, Sadie, just a tap.'

'Not a lot of money. Four pounds.'

'Like I said, it'll be better tonight.'

Tuesday Noon started to sing: 'As the sun goes down on Galway Bay . . .' The girl behind the bar smiled at him and put a finger to her lips. Tuesday Noon nodded. He liked her. He drained his glass and left the bar; he crossed Woodlands Road and sheltered from the rain on the bank under the lime trees, the same bank that during the summer he would use to lie down in the afternoon and sleep. It was about 4.0 p.m., he thought. He stood, turned his collar up against the rain and waited.

Presently the young man and his girl, Sadie, came out of

the bar and turned right, walking side by side. Tuesday Noon followed them, keeping on the far side of the road. The couple turned right and walked up the dark narrow canyon of Park Street and left on to Great Western Road. Tuesday Noon followed them, about one hundred feet behind.

The couple crossed Great Western Road.

Tuesday Noon didn't, but increased his pace until he drew level with them.

They turned right into Belmont Street.

Tuesday Noon stood on the far side of Great Western Road and watched them enter a semi-derelict house on Belmont Street, close to the junction of Great Western Road.

'Reckon that's worth a drink, Mr Montgomerie,' he said.

CHAPTER 9

Thursday, 18.00–Friday 11.30 hours

'Sorry, I get emotional,' said Veronica Bentley. 'I don't know why, I'm not fond of them, but perhaps it's other things as well. A lot of things coming to a head all at once.'

'No problem.' Donoghue took his pipe from his pocket. 'Do you mind if I smoke?'

'Not at all.' Veronica Bentley glanced round the interview room: an orange hard-wearing carpet, a table, black metal legs, polished veneer surface, on which stood a machine for tape-recording interviews; a large red Scottish Police Federation calendar pinned to the wall, and below and to one side a smaller blue calendar issued by the Police Mutual Insurance Company; a window, tall and narrow, which opened only an inch or two and looked out on to the car park at the rear of the police station. 'I imagine that the walls in this room have heard a few stories,' she said.

'Oh, they have.' Donoghue played the flame of his lighter over the tobacco in his pipe. 'I hope that they are going to hear another.'

'Of course. I'll tell you what I can, but I really don't know much about Shane and Eddie. It's difficult to describe, but, well to be perfectly frank, it wasn't really me that was in there, it was my body. But not me. You really have to be an addict to know what I mean.'

'Perhaps. But I think I can understand.'

'It's—they say, what we say—it's our body that's doing it, not ourselves; you got to reach that level of detachment. Whether you're breaking into people's homes if you're a guy, or if you're letting strange men do strange things to you if you're a woman, it's the same attitude, anything for money to buy smack with. So I met Eddie in a café in Byres Road, I scored from him. Just experimenting at first. I met him again, I scored again. He became a pusher, it was just after Christmas, January it started, right at the beginning of term. Pretty soon I had used up my allowance and I needed heroin so he suggested how I could get more.'

'By moving in with him?'

'Basically, yes.' She drew breath and shuddered. 'I guess it's something that I shall have to learn to live with, just another incident in a catalogue of incidents which will make me squirm with embarrassment in the years to come. Or maybe it will make me flush with anger.'

'That would be healthier. I think that you could feel angry and I don't see why you should feel embarrassed. You can't be seen as anything but a victim.'

'I don't want to be patronized, Mr Donoghue. So I moved in to their damp and dingy squat. Eddie gave me heroin and when he hadn't any, I got it from Shane and did the same with Shane that I did with Eddie. It didn't really matter which one was squashing me on the mattress so long as I got a fix. I think I'll take an Aids test.'

'Might be a good idea. If you've got it you've got it, but at least you'll know.'

'It was my gutter. You know, alcoholics talk about their gutter, everyone reaches his own personal gutter. We live in tenements mostly, in this town, and it may well be that your floor is another man's ceiling, but your gutter is your gutter, no matter what or where it is. But ceilings and floors aside, I don't think I could have sunk much lower in real terms. What I came from, you've seen the house, a private education at a day school, a place at University in the Law Faculty, a glittering future; from that to skipping in the nude from one mattress to another in a crumbling, rat-infested squat which was also overrun with mice.' She paused and glanced out of the window as a police vehicle drew into the car park. 'You know, I didn't even like Eddie or Shane; basically they were both neds; they didn't even look good, reminded me of a pair of sparrows, so thin and pale. If you bled them, they couldn't get any whiter. Talk about the Possilpark tan! You know, there was another girl in the building, an Irish lassie called Sadie Kelly, really petite. You could put her in a school uniform and send her off to the third year and nobody would question her. She used to go up to the town and work the street. The only difference between me and Sadie was that I knew the identity of the "clients" and she didn't. She took money and I was paid in kind. They really controlled me; they didn't give me the powder, they used to give me a full syringe, but the longer I stayed, the fix got weaker, so I had to work harder to get what I needed. They kept me strung out and would give me just enough to stop me crawling up the wall.'

Donoghue sucked and blew on his pipe—let the person talk, there's plenty of time to get the vital information—but in his mind he was already drawing up the charge of murder against David Bentley, father of Veronica. There was no need to browbeat, no need to force the pace, just sit back and listen. The blank spaces were being filled in neatly and evenly. There was all the time in the world.

'They were a bit cruel. A lot cruel, really. Eddie told me that my father was his solicitor. I didn't like that. I don't like my father, but he's the only one I've got and I didn't like people laughing at him and me. Far less do I like people laughing at both of us.'

'Shane told us that they kept that information from you.'

Veronica shook her head slowly.

'Well, as the lady once said, he would, wouldn't he? You see, Shane's in the pokey, he's trying to ingratiate himself with you. Eddie sniggered at me pretty well openly, waved letters from my father's firm in front of my eyes; me sitting huddled in a corner waiting for my next fix, and him saying, "Guess who I've just been to see?" Shane did the same, went to my father and came home to me. Eddie told him to do it. Believe me, Mr Donoghue, they were a couple of sickos; they enjoyed going to see my father on any pretext and went home to bounce his daughter. Sometimes they went together and came back together, if you see what I mean.'

Donoghue was silent for a moment, then said. 'Eventually you left the squat?'

She nodded. 'You can remain detached for only so long. I went to see my father. Ironic, really, that I should have gone to see him, but he controls me, he has this "pull", this influence which is not just fatherly, it's more than that. I can't describe it, but he was still controlling me.'

'I don't understand.'

'He's weird. He controls people, he controls my mother, he controls me; when he's not controlling people, he tramples all over them. I thought it was normal. I didn't grow up any other way; only one set of parents in a remote house. I thought all fathers were like that, a bit like God, all-knowing, all-seeing, all-controlling. He certainly controlled my mother.'

'Violently?'

'Sometimes. But it's really on an abstract level that he operates. He just has a way of drawing people to him and controlling them—that is, the people in his private life. Apparently he was always like that, even as a little boy in Northern Ireland. I seemed to wake up when I started university. It was as though I had been parcelled up with string and sealing wax with a label which said, "I've got her this far, you take her the rest of the way and send her back when you've finished." He assumed I was going to join him in the practice. I don't think it occurred to him that I'd leave him.'

'But people do leave him?' Donoghue settled back in his chair, his pipe was burning to his satisfaction.

144

'All the time in his professional life. Secretaries walk out in tears within hours of starting with him; trainees wishing to serve articles leave as soon as they can. A short time spent with Bentley and Co. is no black mark on anybody's c.v.'

'You paint a damning picture, Miss Bentley.'

'It's probably apposite. I think my father is an evil man, Mr Donoghue. Sometimes, if you see him in the right way, I mean the correct way, well, there's a sort of look in his eyes. The gleam, but they are as impenetrable as steel. They make me go cold.'

Donoghue shuffled in his chair.

'And when I look back on the systematic destruction of my mother . . . When I was a wee girl, I remember her as being a lot stronger than she is now. I think she wanted more children, but my father wouldn't allow it.'

'I'm sorry.'

'Well, she's out of it now. We both are. It's going to be tough for the first few months. I know what Homeless Persons' accommodation is like. Eventually she'll get a divorce and a financial settlement but not for a long time. She's got no skills or training. I've got nothing, so it's welfare payments and council land for us.'

'So she's going for a divorce?'

'That's what we were talking about before you came in and asked her to wait outside. That's what gutters are like, so easy to step into, comfortable to stay in, but getting out is one day at a time. When you fall, you fall at terminal velocity and inch your way out.'

'Not everybody makes it at the first attempt, either.'

'Don't say that!' The young woman smiled. She was pale and drawn but Donoghue could see a beautiful woman waiting to blossom from what, at the moment, was a physical wreck. A better diet, a little more flesh on her bones, a sparkle instead of a dullness of the eye . . . that's all that was needed.

'I think you'll make it first go.'

'Thanks for that vote of confidence. I think if somebody, anybody, has faith in you, then you can do almost anything.'

145

'Tell me about your father's place of work.'

'It's an office, like any other.'

'Frankly, in my experience, one office is not like another.'

'It's in an old building on Bath Street, Charing Cross end, quite near here, really. In its heyday the building would have been the home of a wealthy man and his family, with the servants' quarters in the basement. You know the bars on the basement windows of old houses which make the basements a pure fire trap. I always thought that they were there to keep burglars from getting in; in fact, they were designed to stop the servants sneaking out and going on the town. Did you know that?'

'In fact I did,' Donoghue replied. 'I'm something of an aficionado of Glasgow's Victorian architecture. Glasgow is the most Victorian city in the UK in terms of its architectural heritage.'

'Yes,' she mused, 'yes, it probably is.'

'So, your father's office?'

'He has the basement and ground floor of the building. There's a firm of accountants above him; a firm of property surveyors above that, and the attic is the operational base for a private detective. One man and a secretary. Her makes a living by sitting in his car outside houses spying on extra-marital affairs. It's a seedy way of making a penny.'

'Car parking is a problem in that part of town. Can't keep feeding the meters.'

'Daddy has a garage at the rear of the office. It's a rough and ready affair, but it keeps the precious Bentley dry.' She smiled. 'It keeps both Bentleys happy. The garage was thrown up before the present building regulations came into force. It wouldn't be allowed now; it spoils the rear line of the terrace. It's by no means the only one, there are others, all of the same vintage. About twenty years old.'

'So it's just a shelter with an earth floor?'

'Oh no.' Veronica Bentley seemed affronted. 'No, it's got a proper concrete floor and one that's just as filthy greasy as you'd expect after twenty years' constant use. It's fairly oily as well. Daddy had a car once, a Daimler with a porous sump which dripped oil wherever he left it standing. The

146

garage floor never recovered from that. Then Daddy had some work done on another car in the garage, so there's bits of metal everywhere.'

'The garage is directly to the rear of the office?'

'Yes. Why are you interested in it? Is it significant?'

'It could be.'

'I'm a little worried that you've been asking a lot of questions about Daddy. Do you suspect him of some crime?'

'Yes, I do, frankly. I would be lying if I said otherwise. But this is early days, really. I shall have a very open mind.'

'I'm pleased to hear it.' A note of ice in her voice, a trace of haughtiness, a hint of a privileged background. A background that's always there; even in the gutter.

'Tell me, that day that you left the squat for one day, the day you saw your father—what occurred between you?'

Veronica Bentley looked sideways and downwards. 'A row,' she said softly.

'Where?'

'In his office. We must have been heard by everybody. Even the private dick in the attic, let alone all the employees of Bentley and Co. How embarrassing. It was the first time that I had stood up to him, the only time so far. I went home shortly after that and he locked me up in the garden shed.'

'In the garden shed?'

'Well, he made it warm and comfortable, a bed, blankets. I was warm and dry so long as I stayed there and didn't escape by breaking a window and climbing out. I was only allowed thin cotton pyjamas. Daddy said I had to stay there until the poison was out of my system. My mother brought me three meals a day and emptied the slop bucket. And I got the *Glasgow Herald* each morning except Sunday, when it was the *Sunday Telegraph*. I was allowed to move into the house that day that you called for the first time. Daddy thought that the worst was over by then.'

'I see. The row which took place between you and your father—what did you say to him?'

'What didn't I say!'

147

'Well, you see what I'm driving at, Miss Bentley, is, was there anything that was said which could have told your father where it was that you were living?'

A look of horror and sudden realization flashed across Veronica Bentley's eyes. 'Oh . . . oh . . .' she gasped. 'No . . . I know he can be bad . . . but not that bad. You don't think . . .'

'I don't think anything, Miss Bentley. Not at the present. At the present we are still in the process of turning over stones.'

Veronica Bentley nodded. 'Well, yes, I told him where I was living. I mean, not in so many words . . . but I lost the place, as they say, I said something along the lines of, "If you hadn't been such an animal, then I wouldn't now have to break up my body like bread and share it out among your clients so that I can puncture myself four times a day." I knew I'd scored a point because that registered with him, he looked stunned, he looked like he'd been shot in the head, right between the eyes.'

'So all he had to do was look up his files, find two or any clients with the same address, same mode of life, who lived near each other or similar . . .'

'Or similar. It would have been easy, really, especially since Eddie and Shane called on him together on occasions and he would have put two and two together. He's bad but not stupid, and he would have realized who I was living with and then he'd realize why they called to see him on any pretext. He'd realize not just what they were doing but that they were laughing at him while they were doing it. He may even have got the private dick upstairs to do a bit of sleuthing for him.'

'Simple, really.'

'Dead simple,' said Veronica Bentley.

Richard King entered Donoghue's office.

'Ah.' Donoghue glanced up. 'Come in, Richard, take a seat, please.'

King sat. He was fresh-faced, fully rested and ready for the back shift. It was 17.15 hours.

148

'It looks like I'll be home on time for once today,' said Donoghue. 'That will please my lady wife; please me as well, give me time with my children. I just don't see them and they don't see me. So, to business! There's a few things I have to hand over to you in the Eddie Wroe murder, one or two things to be done on your shift.'

'Very good, sir.'

'Well, to come to the point, all roads are leading to Rome. Or rather, all fingers are pointing towards David Bentley.'

'Oh.'

'Yes. Shane Dodemaide's prints on the knife found next to Eddie Wroe's body have been explained. Bentley turns out to be solicitor for both Dodemaide and Wroe. He calls Dodemaide for an interview, about nothing in the event, but during which he says, "Would you mind handing me that knife?" and pointedly doesn't touch it once Dodemaide has carried it safely across Bentley's office and dutifully laid it on the man's desk.'

'I see.'

'So I think Bentley stabbed Wroe with an identical knife, which he subsequently disposed of and which we will never find, and smeared Wroe's blood on the knife with Dodemaide's prints all over it, reverse way on, but all over it none the less and left that knife close to the body.'

'Where it was found.'

'He called Eddie Wroe into his office and took him to the garage at the rear of his house, probably on the pretext of offering him a lift home, but in fact to kill him. The body lay on the floor of the garage which Veronica Bentley informs me is covered with oil and metal filings and not swept clean like a suburban garage. Eddie Wroe's body lay in the garage from midday Saturday to early Sunday morning, by which time rigor mortis had set in. Bentley returned to the locus on Sunday morning, broke the rigor of the corpse, probably bundled it into the boot of his car. Easily done: the deceased was smallish and Bentley is hugely built; he took it half a mile away and dumped it and the knife in the alleyway where they were found.'

'Motive?'

149

'He blamed them for turning his daughter into a smack-head. He also found they forced her to sleep with them for heroin.'

'That would annoy any father.'

'To say the least. But any father would have dragged his daughter home or to hospital and then gone and sorted out Dodemaide and Wroe with a baseball bat and would do so in an uncontrollable temper. Our man lets his daughter return for a few more days of puncture and rape while he lays a convoluted plan to murder one and fit the other up for it. It's that element of detachment, a sense that the injustice is done to him, not his daughter, that I find impossible to fathom.'

'Chilling.'

Donoghue reached forward and took a sheet of paper from his in-tray. 'This is a warrant to search the premises of David Bentley and Co. It includes outbuildings. What I'd like you to do is to get the Forensic chemist, the chap with the glasses—'

'Bothwell.' King glanced at his watch. 'I'll be able to catch him before he leaves for home.'

'Good. Him and a scene of crime officer are to photograph the garage. Let Bothwell loose; we're looking for Wroe's fingerprints in the garage, blood and hair and clothing fibres. Dr Kay is waiting at the Forensic Science Laboratory to match if she can anything that you can supply her with. If the samples match, you can proceed and crave a warrant for the arrest of David Bentley. If you get a warrant, don't exercise it. He's not going anywhere. No one else is in danger and I want to be there when he's arrested.'

'Very good, sir.'

'I should also tell you that I've asked for permission for firearms to be drawn. Bentley has a pair of revolvers in his library. I don't for one minute think he'll shoot it out with the police, but I want to be prepared for any eventuality.'

'I dare say if we don't take guns, we'll only need them.'

'And if we do take them, we won't need them, which is how we all would prefer it. Please pass all this on to

150

Montgomerie. He's drawn the graveyard shift, as you know. If we have grounds for a warrant, he'll exercise it with me.'

A uniformed officer jemmied off the padlock of the garage and the doors swung outwards. It proved to be a roomy garage with a workbench at the further end, a metal cabinet to the left, a skylight and a naked light-bulb hanging from a metal beam. Wide tyres from a large car had left greasy impressions on the oily surface.

Elliot Bothwell stood patiently holding his case while the scene of crime officer set up the camera and the flash equipment. He watched with interest. Even in these days of high tech photography with lifelike colour prints, the police preferred black and white photography. It had been explained to him once, colour flattens a scene, black and white is more three-dimensional in effect. Elliot Bothwell was thirty-six years old and he remembered that he should have phoned home to tell his mother he would be late for supper. He looked around the garage. His eye was drawn to the far corner, close to where the metal cabinet stood. Richard King came and stood beside him.

'Somewhere in there, Mr Bothwell,' said King, 'is a place where we believe a body to have lain; so any blood you find and fingerprints, hair, clithing, fibres . . .'

'It lay over there, sir.' Bothwell nodded his head towards the metal cabinet. He repeated the movement. It annoyed King, he found it a lazy, perfunctory movement. A raised and pointed arm would have seemed more enthusiastic, more professional, but two slow, sure nods of a thick-jowled head irritated him.

'How do you know?'

'Well, you can see the footprints in the oil that lead from the door here to the corner over there.'

'There are footprints all over the garage floor.'

'Yes, sir.' Bothwell blinked. 'Both those prints walk from the door to the corner and then return. The person who made the prints is well built, you can tell that by the size of the print. He walked to the corner from the door carrying nothing. You can tell that because the feet are pointed slightly outwards, as are normal footprints.'

'Go on.' King was intrigued and was no longer annoyed by Bothwell's laziness of gesture.

'Well, on the return journey, he was carrying something, because his feet were planted parallel with each other, that is, the toes pointed dead ahead, not outwards. That's a sure sign of someone carrying something heavy. The other footprints in the garage, they're various sizes, big and small, facing each other, facing in the same direction, widely spaced. It's as though one person had chased another around the garage at some point.'

King smiled at Bothwell. 'I'll leave it to you.'

The flash gun popped.

If you can control it, then it's all right. In fact, it's pretty good. Malcolm Montgomerie had resisted alcohol that morning, had enjoyed six hours of good, nourishing alcohol-free sleep. He awoke at 7.0 p.m., had a coffee, showered, enjoyed a ready-cooked meal at 9.0 p.m. and soaked up television until 10.45 when he pulled on his ski-jacket and told himself that alcohol, if you can control it, is pretty good stuff. He left his flat, went down the common stair, into his car and drove to P Division. He entered the rear entrance of the police station, signed in, checked his pigeonhole, and was about to ascend the stair to the CID corridor when the desk officer called him back.

'Yes?' said Montgomerie.

'Someone to see you, sir,' said the officer. 'Out in the front reception area.'

'Who?'

The desk officer shrugged and smiled. Montgomerie walked to the desk, lifted the hinged section, walked into the uniform bar and glanced into the public area. Tuesday Noon sat on one of the black upholstered seats next to a plant in a large white bowl. He glanced up at Montgomerie and smiled. 'I've got something that's worth a drink, Mr Montgomerie,' he said.

The uniformed desk officer watched as Montgomerie

spoke with Tuesday Noon for a minute or two. He then saw Montgomerie take out his wallet and hand the aged derelict two five-pound notes. The aged derelict kept his hand open and held Montgomerie's gaze. Montgomerie paused and then pushed a third five-pound note into the man's hand. The elderly man shuffled out of the building, leaving a sour smell in his wake. Montgomerie went upstairs to the CID corridor and the bar officer took a can of ozone-friendly air freshener and sprayed the public area. Liberally.

Montgomerie skipped up the stairs two at a time and strode purposefully into the office he shared with King and Abernethy.

'The footfall of a confident man,' said King, not looking up from his desk.

'Well, wouldn't you be confident, a solid day's sleep, not fifteen seconds inside the building and your grass lays gold dust on you.'

'Gold dust is falling out of the sky.' King put his pen down and looked up. 'There've been major developments in the Wroe case.'

'Oh?' Montgomerie walked to the table in the corner of the room and spooned instant coffee into a mug. 'Coffee?'

'No, thanks. I'm awash with the liquid.'

'So tell I?' Montgomerie poured boiling water from the geyser into the mug and added milk.

'All indications are that Bentley senior is the culprit.'

'Veronica's father?' Montgomerie raised his eyebrows.

'The one and the same. His name just kept popping up in all the wrong places or all the right places, depending on your point of view.'

'It pops up more often than you think,' said Montgomerie, and told King that Tuesday Noon had reported seeing David Bentley burning rubber in his Bentley, tearing down Bath Street, shooting red lights at 7.0 a.m. Sunday last.

'You'd better sober him up, then,' said King. 'It looks as though he's going to be a Crown witness. May not need him, though.' King tapped the report that he was writing. 'We got the results on blood traces and hair and fingerprints that Elliot Bothwell found in Bentley's garage, the one behind his place of work. Dr Kay confirms that they belong to the deceased.'

'Certainly seems like he's got some explaining to do.' Montgomerie sat at his desk. 'What was the motive?' King told him. 'So on that basis, and the evidence, I requested a warrant for his arrest and arranged the release of Dodemaide.'

'You're going to pick him up tonight?'

'No, you and Fabian are going to pick him up tomorrow. He probably thought that you could do with the overtime.'

Montgomerie groaned. 'Anything lying to be done?'

'Nothing. Why, you anxious to work or something?'

'In a sense, yes.' Montgomerie sipped his coffee. 'I've got a visit to make, I have some gold dust to sweep up.'

Montgomerie drove to the squat on Belmont Street. The rain had eased off but had not completely stopped, and a dark cloud, low and foreboding and visible in the darkness, spoke of an impending deluge. Behind him was a van containing two male officers and WPC Willems. At the front door of the squat Montgomerie made to knock, then he paused, hunched his shoulder and burst the door open. It was locked, nominally: a single barrel lock in a rotten door in a rotten frame. It gave easily.

They found Sadie Kelly and Nicholas McQueen lying on the same mattress, under the same blanket. They blinked as Montgomerie switched the light on.

'Wakey, wakey!' he said.

'Do you have a warrant?' said McQueen with an imperiousness that all the cops found comical, but only Elka Willems couldn't stifle a laugh.

'Do we need one?' Montgomerie glanced around the room. Dirty clothing lay in two piles on either side of the mattress. A cardboard box contained other clothing. 'Get dressed. We're taking you for a nice ride to the police station. We'd like to talk to you about knocking two old ladies down and stealing the princely sum of four pounds.'

154

'How did you know it was us?' Sadie Kelly blinked and sounded genuinely puzzled.

Nicholas McQueen lay back and pulled the blanket over his head, making a low moaning sound as he did so.

'I knew you'd come,' said Bentley, sitting in the armchair. 'So I stayed home. Half-expected you yesterday, in fact. Stayed home yesterday as well. Wouldn't look too clever, being arrested in front of my staff.'

'I can understand that,' Donoghue replied, sitting opposite Bentley.

A clock ticked.

Donoghue and Montgomerie had first gone to Bentley's office in Bath Street and, on being told that he had not come in that day, they had driven out to Balfron, to Bentley's home. They were followed by a marked police car and a police van. The convoy pulled to a halt noisily on the gravel in front of Bentley's house. Donoghue got out of his Rover and looked at the building. David Bentley stood at the library window, looking at the officers. He was dressed casually in white slacks and a blue jersey, light blue to match his car which was parked at the side of the house. Donoghue stood and looked at Bentley. For a few seconds the men stared at each other, holding each other's gaze. Then Bentley slowly nodded his head.

Moments later, he opened the front door of the house and bade the police enter. 'I think I know why you're here,' he said.

'Good.' Donoghue swept his homburg off as he stepped over the threshold. He was pleased that this was going to be a civilly conducted arrest, unemotional and restrained. 'That is going to save us both difficulty.'

'Perhaps I could have a word with you in the drawing-room?'

'We can do all the necessary talking at the police station, Mr Bentley.'

'Please. One minute is all I ask.'

'Very well, but Mr Montgomerie will accompany me.'

'Is that necessary?'

'I'm indulging you as it is, Mr Bentley.'

In the drawing-room, which Donoghue found stood on the opposite side of the hallway to the library in which he and Bentley had first encountered each other, Bentley insisted that Donoghue and Montgomerie sat down. He also sat. Donoghue sensed Montgomerie's impatience, but he was curious about Bentley. He wanted to hear what he had to say. The man intrigued him, dangerously so, and he was reminded of Dr Cass's reference to spiders: their webs, their jaws.

'No,' said Bentley, 'it would really look too bad if I was arrested at work. So I waited at home.'

'Didn't think of making a run for it?'

'From where to where?' Bentley relaxed a little in the chair and he caught Donoghue's eye with a gentle gleam in his own eyes.

Donoghue shuddered.

'You know, Mr Donoghue, I felt that there was an affinity between us from the moment I met you. You and I had an instant rapport; a certain awareness. Like brothers. Now I feel a sense of something lost. I glimpsed something that might have been. It may still be.'

'I do not share your faith in that respect, Mr Bentley.'

'A pity. But do try to keep an open mind. I shall, of course, be pleading not guilty. I shall fight all the way, point by point, technicality by technicality, and I shall enjoy it. I see you as a worthy adversary, Mr Donoghue.'

'It won't be me you'll be fighting.'

'No, it will be the officer of the Procurator Fiscal, but his case will depend on your report. You know, many a policeman has left the force to pursue a successful career as a criminal lawyer. It's just a question of contacts.'

'I'm happy in my work,' said Donoghue.

'And your friend?' Bentley smiled at Montgomerie.

'Just what do you want to say to us, Mr Bentley?' Donoghue asked icily. 'Gentlemanly conduct is one thing, but we will not be trifled with.'

'Well, as I say, I shall be pleading "not guilty", but just for argument's sake—'

'We haven't time to argue.' Donoghue's expression hardened. 'This is public money that's ticking on the meter here.'

'For the sake of argument, if I did kill that boy, what's lost?'

'A human life. That's loss enough for anybody.'

'He might have been taking my daughter's life. A man has to protect his own. Besides, he was a cheap, useless ned; he would have died anyway, he had limited life-expectancy. Neds do, it's their mode of life. If I hadn't killed him, for argument's sake, if I hadn't killed him, someone else would.'

'And just for argument's sake, what about Shane Dodemaide; who, just for the sake of argument, might have been wrongly and deliberately implicated in the murder of his mate?'

'Mate, you say. People like that can't form relationships. They take the body of a girl, somebody's daughter, and share it among themselves.' Anger rose in Bentley's voice and subsided quickly. 'Perhaps I might have been doing him a favour.'

'Some favour. Ten years in the pokey doesn't sound like a favour to me.'

'He wouldn't have been a heroin addict when he came out. And he would have been alive. He would have had a greater life-expectancy in the gaol than in the streets. He would have had a lot to thank me for.'

'Thin ice on which to erect a defence.' Donoghue stood. 'I think this conversation is concluded.'

Bentley smiled land stood. 'I think it is. I'll just get my coat. It's in the library.'

'Do not do anything rash,' said Donoghue. 'My men are in the hall and also outside the house.'

'I have no intention of doing anything rash.' Bentley left the drawing-room, leaving the door open as he did so.

Donoghue turned to Montgomerie. 'I was curious,' he said by way of explanation. 'Curious as to what he had to—'

The single gunshot echoed in the house.

Montgomerie saw Donoghue close his eyes, as if reproaching himself for some act of monumental stupidity. There was a clatter of running feet in the hall.

Silence.

The uniformed sergeant stepped into the drawing-room. He looked towards Donoghue, lost for words.

Donoghue opened his eyes and stood. '... rarely commit suicide,' he said.

'Pardon, sir?' Montgomerie stood.

'Nothing.' Donoghue began to walk to the door. 'I just didn't think he'd do that. Didn't think he'd do that at all.'